CHRISTMAS
ON THE
FJORD

CHRISTMAS ON THE FJORD

Elle Thrasher

Ebook ISBN: 979-8-9855971-7-2

Paperback ISBN: 979-8-9903433-1-3

For information: elle@ellethrasher.com

Cover Designer: Damonza

Editor: Aimee Vance, Revel Books

To the readers who've always wanted to visit Norway during the festive season.

God Jul!

CONTENT NOTICE

For a full list of content warnings, please visit the author's website.

www.ellethrasher.com/christmas-on-the-fjord

PRONUNCIATION GUIDE

Espen -- Ess-pen

Øyvin -- Oy-vihn

Balder -- Bahl-derr

Bente -- Ben-teh

Dagny -- Dahg-nee

Fjell -- Fyell

Freija -- Frey-ah

God Jul – Gooh Yuhl

Halvar -- Hal-vahr

Jorunn -- Yoo-runn

Leif -- Layf

Nisse – Niss-eh

Oddvar -- Odd-vahr

Skolvik -- Skoll-veek

Solveig -- Sool-vay

Torsten -- Torr-sten

Trygve -- Tryg-veh

Ylva -- Yll-vah

1

LENNIE

I stretched my arms above my head, fingers grazing the wood headboard as a cozy warmth enveloped me from both sides. Not an ounce of sunlight streamed in through the curtains, but that wasn't surprising—sunrise in mid-December in Norway was after 8 a.m. and full daylight only lasted from nine until three in the afternoon. What *was* surprising was that I was the first one awake.

Rolling onto my side and bringing my arms back under my duvet, I stared at Espen—normally, the early riser—and watched as sleep relaxed his features, a smile still perpetually plastered across his face. His dark hair fell over one eye, giving him a childlike innocence I couldn't help but admire. No matter where we were, including here in Øyvin's bedroom, the centuries-old fae always seemed at ease.

Øyvin on the other hand... Well, the Asshole was forever slightly grumpy and testing my nerves, but I paid him back in kind by getting into trouble as often as I could. I shifted to my back and looked at the Fjord Fae on my other side. His blond hair was mussed up and his short lashes barely brushed across his cheeks, Espen's opposite in every way.

"Are you going to stare all morning?"

I startled at the question, but he didn't see it, his eyes still firmly shut. "Wasn't sure you were alive. You sleep like a log."

Øyvin opened his eyes and gave me a challenging look, those blues swallowed by the darkness of his pupils. "At least I don't thrash around like a fish caught in a net."

"Perhaps I needed saving from a bad dream?" Not true. I had a very pleasant *yoga* dream last night where they had me in all kinds of positions, one of which was a modified version of bridge pose that I was *very* interested in testing out some time soon.

"Espen can save you," he said, rolling out of bed and sauntering across the room in nothing but a pair of boxers that clung to his muscular thighs.

"Uh-huh," I muttered, bewitched by the Fjord Fae's ass. Despite his surly personality, or maybe to make up for it, Øyvin was the most attractive male I'd ever seen and it was hard to look away. "Sure."

Øyvin threw a knowing look over his shoulder before he grabbed his clothes for the day and headed to the bathroom.

Espen meanwhile, nestled up against my side, kissing me on the shoulder as he murmured, "I'll save you. Always."

My heart stuttered and I brushed my fingers through his luscious dark-brown locks. He let out a low moan and scooted even closer, his body now firmly tucked against me.

I didn't know how the three of us had fallen into such a comfortable living arrangement—residing primarily at Øyvin's since returning from Ohio, even having dinners together when they weren't working late—but, surprisingly, I didn't mind it. I'd never been one for any sort of long-term relationships, placing high value on my freedom and independence. With each passing day, these two slowly chipped away at that resolve, and while it was scary, I also kind of liked it.

Whatever this situationship currently was, it made me happy. There wasn't any loss of independence like I'd felt in relationships before in the US. Here in Norway, I didn't feel like Espen and Øyvin were tying me down to a particular lifestyle. Already, this arrangement felt so much better than my old life.

My connection to them wasn't holding me back from the things I wanted most: adventure, spontaneity, family and friends. I could have those things and more. I could do what I wanted, when I wanted to. New powers and fae-ness aside, my life now felt rife with opportunity and I wasn't going to let go of that. Especially after I'd spent the better part of my 28 years searching for it, even if I hadn't known exactly what *it* would look like.

I was ready to *live,* and these men made me feel alive.

As I prepared my morning oatmeal, throwing some chocolate chips and cinnamon on top to liven it up, Espen stepped up behind me in his police uniform and wrapped his arms around my torso. Nuzzling into my neck, he murmured, "Have I mentioned how much I like living with you?"

I couldn't help but smile at the sentiment and my body flushed from his proximity, the spoon in my hand shaking softly. That these men still affected me so easily after a month with them was both exasperating and thrilling.

"Well," I started, a teasing tone in my voice. "Do you like me less since you haven't moved in full-time?"

He chuckled against my neck, the vibrations sending goosebumps down my arms. Stepping back, he let out a deep sigh and I looked over my shoulder to see his eyes roving over my sweatshirt and leggings combo, leaving a tantalizing warmth in their wake. "There's a lot to like. Especially when you wear these." He pinched my butt.

I let out an undignified squeak and dropped the spoon into the bowl. "You mean my leggings?" I wiggled my ass, showing off the tight black material, and he pinched me again, this time a little harder, and let out a low groan.

"Yes," he replied, his voice thick and heavy. "You should wear these all the time."

"Will you pinch my butt every time I wear them?" I spun around and leaned against the kitchen counter, the cool stone biting into my lower back.

Espen looked ravenous, his pupils blown wide, a flush to his cheeks, his lips slightly wet like he'd swiped his tongue across them. "I'll want to touch your ass every single time you put those on."

I scrunched my face like I was repulsed by the prospect of his hands on my ass all the time. I wasn't. "Lighten up on the pinching and we'll be good."

"Fine." His lips quirked into a cheeky grin and he flicked his eyebrows once. "I'll save your ass from too many marks."

"That's my job," Øyvin said, striding into the room and adjusting his thick, cream knit sweater around his broad shoulders. The heated look he gave me sent tingly zings down my spine and I curled my toes. How could he have such an effect on me with one simple look?

"And you do excellent work," I teased, giving him a wink that earned me a slight twitch from the corner of his lips.

"Speaking of jobs, I need to go to mine," Espen said before leaning forward and planting a kiss on my cheek. "I'll see you two later." He bounded over to the front door and yanked on his chunky, black boots. "Don't kill each other while training."

"Training?" I straightened up and crossed my arms over my chest. What had I missed now? Had they told me about this or was this one of Øyvin's throw-her-into-the-deep-end plans? "What training?"

"He'll fill you in," Espen remarked with a quick wave and was out the door in the next instant.

I turned to Øyvin who reached into the fridge and pulled out the carton of eggs. "Care to explain?"

He set the eggs beside the stovetop and rolled up his sleeves. Leaning against the counter a few feet from me, he glanced over and gave me a lopsided grin that had my stomach flip-flopping in a bad way.

"Today you start learning how to hide your ears by yourself."

Ah, shit.

I'd been doing just fine having them help me hide them every morning before they went to work for the last few weeks. I'd tried several times already, but never successfully. Usually, I ended up creating half a mirage that lasted about three seconds and failed to hide the very top points of my ears completely.

"We have four days until Christmas," he added. "So, you have four days to learn."

"Five. We have *five* days until Christmas." Numbers might not have been my forté, but I could count to five.

He shook his head. "In Norway we celebrate Christmas on Christmas Eve. Haven't you been paying attention? Espen is super excited about it."

He wasn't wrong, but Espen was like a puppy who got excited about everything, which I liked about him. I'd been so caught up in trying to learn how to speak and read Norwegian for the last month that my focus was all over the place lately.

"Let me get this straight. You want me to learn how to hide my ears in *four* days? Why the rush?"

He nodded and cracked an egg into the pan on the stove. "Exactly. It can be your Christmas present to us. Plus, there is a caroling event downtown on Christmas Eve that Espen wants to drag us to, which would be a great time to test it out, ergo *rush*."

I groaned and rubbed my hands across my face. There were so many ways this could go wrong. But... Deep down I wanted to learn how to hide my ears by myself. It would also make the guys happy and was, as Halvar, the Fjell Fae Head Guard had once put it, *the basics* of my magic.

I hadn't tested my powers much, just little snippets here and there while the guys were home or on the weekends when we'd head up into the forest away from the village so no one would spot us and I didn't accidentally cause an incident. But even then, we'd only tinkered with the light magic that I'd previously used and avoided anything to do with the Fjell Fae powers—mostly because neither Espen nor Øyvin were Fjell Fae and didn't know what to ask me to do. Rumor had it Halvar was going to train me at some point, but the stoic fae had been busy with Fjell Council business after Queen Freija died and was going to get back to me in the new year. Until then...

I let out a long sigh, knowing I couldn't get out of this. "When do we start?"

"After breakfast. Now, hurry up and eat. We've got a lot to do."

2

LENNIE

After breakfast, I showered and pulled on warmer clothes for the chilly winter day. I swept my long blonde hair up into a ponytail so we could easily see my ears, and brushed my teeth.

I'd slowly made myself at home the last few weeks, buying a new electric toothbrush and toiletries I preferred. I was grateful Øyvin let me move in, but I wasn't naive enough to believe it wasn't in part due to his anxiety that I might reveal myself as fae if I lived anywhere but with him or Espen. With the little knowledge I had of my fae powers so far, I couldn't blame him.

During the days when I hadn't been testing out my powers, I'd been on excursions with my phone, wishing I still had my old DSLR camera. The photos were great, but not the spectacular shots I used to get with my baby that had been destroyed. Losing my camera felt like losing an extension of myself, but I couldn't afford to replace it yet.

I'd also been practicing speaking and reading Norwegian in the past few weeks, and could even say Merry Christmas (*God Jul*) now too. Thankfully, my translation magic still worked and I could understand Norwegian spoken around me, but I was getting frustrated that I couldn't respond in the language myself. Everything was different, even the extra three letters Norwegians had in their alphabet, but I was determined to master it. While the guys were at work, I downloaded apps and watched videos online to teach myself, then practiced each night with them.

I stared at myself in the mirror, studying the pointed ears I'd sported for a whole month as unease gnawed at me. As the vanilla latte, basic-of-basic level of magic, creating a mirage-thing over my new pointy ears shouldn't be too troublesome. In theory.

But, this was me, Lennie Martin. According to Øyvin, Trouble was my middle name. It was actually Louise, but that was neither here nor there.

It was time for me to start truly learning how to use my new powers, not just testing things out like a science experiment to be examined.

"So, how are we going to do this?" I asked as I waltzed into the living room, shoving any worry I felt aside. Water lapped against the hull of the boat in the bay garage, soft light reflecting off the water below the house and shining through the windows by the fireplace in the late morning. Both the piano and fireplace sat dormant, while the checkered throw pillows were neatly set on the leather sofa in the orderly fashion that Øyvin preferred in all aspects of his home. The space was cozy and lived in, but if you looked closely, everything had its place. Even the Christmas decorations. The tree twinkled in the corner beside the black, stove-top style fireplace and paper snowflakes hung in the living room window.

Øyvin stood in the middle of the living room area, pushing aside the coffee table. I helped him move it and set down the small mirror I'd brought from the bathroom, thinking I'd need it to see if the magic was working or not.

"We start simple. Focus on this one task, and avoid any and all distractions."

I pursed my lips at his words. While that wasn't an impossible task, I'd definitely have to close my eyes. The way his cream sweater hugged his shoulders and arms was distracting, especially since I knew in vivid detail what lay beneath the woven fibers.

"Trouble…"

"Yeah." I cleared my throat and straightened up as I entered the space he'd made in front of the couch, shoving aside my sexy thoughts. "I'm here and focused."

"Mm-hmm." His deadpan stare told me he knew exactly where my thoughts were focused.

"I'm serious." I set my hands on my hips, determination setting in under his doubtful gaze. "I can do this." *If I said it out loud, would that make it true? Perhaps even easier?* Worth a shot. "I can totally do this."

He stepped in front of me and flexed his fingers at his sides, like he was trying to tamper his frustration with me or stop himself from reaching forward to touch me. Honestly, with how hot and cold the emotional energy between us vacillated on any given day, either was possible.

"Focus on that well of power, the warmth that sits right here." He pointed to the spot right underneath my boobs in the middle of my chest. "Close your eyes and picture your ears the way they used to look."

"I can't say I ever paid much attention to my ears." *Seriously, who looked at their ears on a regular basis?*

He groaned, and I bit my bottom lip to stifle a laugh. Frustrating Øyvin had quickly become one of my favorite pastimes. He made it entirely too easy.

"Picture your old ears as clearly as you can. Imagine your ears without points."

"Got it." Rounded, fairly normal looking ears, with holes pierced in the lobes for earrings I hardly ever wore. "What next?"

"Now, imagine pulling that warm power up through your spine and deposit some of it at your ears."

That sounded crazy, but crazier shit had happened lately. Like traveling to Norway, accidentally photographing an illegal transfer of magic, and then becoming a demi-fae when a Fjell Fae named Nora decided to commit regicide along with her bat-shit crazy boyfriend, who also happened to be the King of the Fjord Fae.

"Can you do that?" Øyvin asked, crossing his arms and giving me a look that said he had his doubts. Nothing ignited my stubborn streak faster.

"I can do this," I repeated with more conviction as I rolled my shoulders.

He waved his hand, urging me on.

With the picture of my human ears firmly in mind, I closed my eyes, placed my hand on my left shoulder like I'd seen the guys do countless times when using their magic, and focused on the well of power that swirled within my chest. I deepened my breaths, pulling air in through my nose and out through my mouth, relaxing into the posture. Slowly and steadily I pulled tendrils of power through my torso, feeling it glide upward and brush along my spine, then my neck. I let the little lump of power settle at the back of my head, picturing it gathering there before spreading it toward my ears. My breaths grew quicker—

"Steady," Øyvin said, his voice barely a whisper.

I tilted my head from one shoulder and then over to the other, encouraging the magic to disperse evenly. A warm, tingling sensation grew where it moved and a wave of heat swept across my head and down my neck.

I cracked open one eye and peered at Øyvin. His brow furrowed as he stared intently at my ears.

"Anything?" I asked, hoping I'd nailed it on the first try.

"Almost," he replied, his gaze never straying from my head. "Keep going."

I closed my eyes again and pushed harder, pressing the warm power upward. "What about now?"

"Yes!"

My eyes flew open and heat washed down my spine, the power returning to my chest as I raised my hands in victory. *Fucking crushed it.*

Øyvin's smile dropped and his shoulders slumped.

"What?" I reached for the mirror on the coffee table and inspected my ears. Damn it! The pointed tips were still there.

"You had it for a few seconds."

"I doubt that counts as success, though."

He shook his head, and I let out an exasperated sigh.

"It might take some time to hold it for extended periods," he added. "But the more you try, the more you successfully create the mirage, the easier it should become. One day it'll be instinct and you'll barely have to think about it."

"You mean *practice makes perfect?*"

He nodded and crossed his arms. "Building stamina."

"I do have decent stamina." I snapped my fingers and winked, which earned me one of his signature eye rolls.

"How does this mirage thing even work? Is it like when Espen changed my clothes for the ball?" I asked, setting my hands on my hips and recalling how, in the blink of an eye, I'd gone from leggings and a sweater to the gorgeous silver-and-green dress he'd put me in.

"Yes," Øyvin replied, "but mirage may not be the best word for it."

"So, it's more like a shift those wolves did?" That snap-crackle noise their bones had made as they shifted from fae to wolves still haunted my dreams. Seriously, some things you couldn't unhear or unsee, and it was a damn shame those doggos would never vacate my memory.

"Somewhere in between," Øyvin sighed before continuing. "They're evolutionary physical mirages. Think of it like a blanket of magic covering what's truly there. Take that dress of yours. You were wearing your normal clothes underneath, but the magical layer—the dress—was wrapped over you, and the main thing you could feel and touch. It wasn't only the appearance of the clothes, like a mirage, but more tangible than that, even if it was only temporary."

That magic existed was still wild to think about, but his explanation was straightforward. I'd lifted the skirt of my dress and moved about in it as if it were on my body properly, not able to feel the casual clothes underneath. It had *felt* real. "And the ears are the same type of magic?"

Øyvin nodded. "The magic was gifted to all fae by our ancestors to help us hide when the human population started to swell. That was a very long time ago."

I had a feeling 'a long time ago' was many centuries...

"Try again," Øyvin commanded, drawing me back to the present.

I did as requested, focusing on the well of magic in my chest and pulling it up like I'd done before. Again and again and again. Each time I held it for a few seconds longer than the last, but it still wasn't good enough. I needed to hold it for hours, if not a full day, while around humans in town. I couldn't suddenly have it drop while I was at Oddvar's or visiting with Solveig. At the thought of my ears suddenly changing before them, I imagined Oddvar keeling over from a heart attack, and Solveig calling her best friends. Before I'd make it home, the whole town would know thanks to those gossips.

After a bajillion attempts and two cups of coffee for both me and Øyvin, I was ready to give up.

"One more, and then we can be done for today," Øyvin said, mirroring my frustration with my lack of progress. Clearly his patience had a limit, which was decidedly longer than I'd expected.

Clenching my teeth, I pulled the power up my spine again, letting it settle at the top of my neck before dispersing toward my ears. The telltale warmth spread from one side of my head to the other, and I pictured my human ears, willing the mirage-like magic into being.

The shift registered with me and I brushed my fingers across the rounded ends, shuddering at the sensation. Øyvin's brows rose slightly.

"Thousandth time's the charm?"

"Perhaps," Øyvin conceded with a twitch of his lips, which was generous for the grump. "But how long can you hold it?"

"You really don't think I can last long?" I asked, flicking my eyebrows once, my tone filled with challenge.

"No." He took a step closer, testing me. His voice dropped to a low timbre that skated across my skin, leaving goosebumps in its wake. "I really don't."

"Ye of little faith."

His tongue swept over his bottom lip as he stopped a mere inch in front of me, and I couldn't stop myself from tracking the movement. "Trouble by name," he said, the words twisting the muscles in my core. He leaned in, and my entire body tensed at his proximity, his breath skittering across the sensitive skin on my neck and shattering my concentration as my mind shifted to parts of me that were decidedly not my ears. "Trouble by nature."

"You don't play fair."

"Never," he replied, then pulled back, taking the delectable air with him. "But neither will Espen. You really think you can keep it together in public with him leaving little kisses on your cheek or whispering his happy, sweet words in your ear?"

Fuck. The Asshole had a point.

I glanced into the little mirror on the coffee table and, sure enough, thanks to his distraction, my ears had reverted to their pointy demi-fae state.

Øyvin reached out with his thumb and forefinger, tilting my head up so our eyes could meet. "You'll get there eventually, just not with me this morning. I need to head below the surface." He dropped his hand and I shuddered at the loss of his touch, shaking off the heady sensation that had taken up root within me. We were always like this around each other—like a fire that ebbed and flowed from embers to bonfire and back again. It was overwhelming, but part of me didn't mind it one bit.

As he stepped toward the front door and pulled on his boots and jacket, he asked, "What are you doing with the rest of your day?"

I yanked the coffee table back into position in front of the sofa, and sauntered over to the Christmas tree we'd put up in the corner of the living room. The smell of spruce permeated the space, sending all kinds of nostalgia through me. "I'm going to finish decorating the tree," I replied, leaning down to grab the box of ornaments Espen had left for me to finish adding to the branches.

"Sounds cozy," Øyvin said, sounding more like he wanted to run in the other direction than assist, which was fair. Decorating trees wasn't for everyone, and honestly it didn't surprise me considering how grumpy and standoffish Øyvin could be. You'd never find him humming Christmas tunes, watching cheesy Hallmark movies, and donning an ugly sweater while drinking cocoa anytime soon. Espen, on the other hand...

"Espen asked me to finish adding the last of the decorations." I reached into the box of round wooden tree slices with the bark still on the edges, each with festive scenes or sayings burned into them. I pulled a few of them out and did my best to pronounce the Norwegian phrases on them. "This one says *God Jul*. This one says *Jeg Elsker Deg*." Øyvin flinched, but I continued. "And this one says something about *Juletiden*." I glanced over at Øyvin again, hoping I hadn't completely butchered the phrases—the only one I really knew well was *God Jul*. His pupils were blown wide and he looked like he'd seen a ghost.

"Is my Norwegian really that bad?" I looked back at the ornaments, trying to remember my lessons to recognize any of the words. Had I offended him? Accidentally called his grandmother ugly? Besmirched his ancestors?

He shook his head and brushed his hand across the light stubble on his chin. "It's not atrocious."

I beamed and gave myself an imaginary pat on the back. "Step in the right direction, then."

He nodded, looked at the door, and then back at me.

"You all right there? Forgetting something?" I asked, narrowing my eyes at his hesitation.

"Yeah, I'm fine." He nodded again, then grabbed the handle and sauntered out the door.

"Not even a goodbye," I chuckled to myself as I pulled more ornaments out of the box and set them down on the coffee table. Like the wooden tree slices, all of them were made of natural materials, including straw reindeer and little knitted mittens. It was cute and cheerful, and a far cry from the shiny rainbow baubles and tinsel I'd grown up with on my parent's Christmas tree.

With a contented sigh, I put some festive music on my phone and started merrily decorating our tree.

3

ØYVIN

Jeg elsker deg.

Those three words had just left Lennie's lips without a single care in the world, as if they meant nothing. From her lack of reaction, it was obvious she had no idea what she'd just said, only reading the words on the ornament, but *I* knew what they meant. I paced outside the front door of the boathouse, desperately needing to get to work, but unable to jump into the fjord, surprised by my own reaction to the simple phrase.

The sun hid behind a thick cloud cover, lending a dull glow to the street and water. While it hadn't snowed yet—and we usually didn't get snow until January and February—there'd been enough chilly days and the scent of snow in the air on several occasions, signaling winter's imminent arrival.

Christmas music started inside, Lennie singing along as some woman belted out what she *really* wanted underneath the tree.

Jeg elsker deg.

The words rang in my head, burning a hole through my defenses. She hadn't meant to say it, and I knew she didn't mean it yet. She'd made it perfectly clear she wasn't ready for "labels", and I wasn't ready to define anything either. What we had, what we were doing, clearly had all three of us happy, so there was no need to rock the boat or upend our joy. At least, not beyond what Espen had planned, which I wholly agreed with, and hoped she would, too. Not just for her own sake, but for the fae.

I shook my shoulders, trying to shake off the shock that had set in. Even in her muddled Norwegian, those twelve letters had still knocked the air out of my lungs. I vigorously brushed my hands through my hair, making a mess of it, and headed for the water, hoping a cold dip and the swim to the Fjord Fae palace would clear my racing thoughts.

Do I want her to mean those words?

Do I want to say them back?

It'd been over a century since I'd uttered those three words, and that had ended poorly. So much so, that I'd devoted myself wholly to the fjord and my career. That is... until Lennie missed her boat and brought her chaos into my life.

She has no idea.

I shook my head and dove into the fjord.

4

LENNIE

Training with Øyvin had left me hungry, both for food and for success in this new endeavor. After I decorated the tree, I spent the rest of my Wednesday practicing the ear magic in front of the bathroom mirror and quizzing myself on food items we had in the fridge, trying to say the names for them in Norwegian.

Thursday morning I wandered over to Oddvar's café to grab lunch with Espen before we went to the woods for a quick practice session during his break. Even though I'd been here for weeks, the sight of Skolvik was still magical, even more so as Christmas neared. Most of the buildings were white, but some had been painted a sunny yellow or traditional, Norwegian red. Residences and businesses alike had decorated for the holidays. Wreaths hung on doors and bunches of oat sheaves to feed the birds were fastened to porches with red ribbon. Some windows had a single light-up star hanging in them, while others had seven tiered candles on a wooden triangle-base lighting their windowsills. The Christmas decorations in Norway were beautiful and simple, and miles different from the inflatable Santas and light up reindeer you'd find in the US.

A cold breeze zipped across the fjord and into town, leaving the village slightly frosty. The overcast skies lent the whole place an eerie ambiance, as if we were cocooned in a chilly blanket. I'd bundled up in layers, my jacket, and my scarlet-and-gray hat. While the hat covered my ears, Espen also used his magic this morning to hide the tips.

Surprisingly, I arrived at Oddvar's before Espen. He was usually early to everything, but I didn't allow myself to worry. He was probably caught up saying hello to everyone he passed between the police station and the café. Seizing the moment alone, I strolled across the café and rested my forearm on the counter where Oddvar, the owner, stood awaiting customers, ready to ask the question I'd been thinking about for weeks.

"So, Oddvar," I tapped the counter, "any chance you have a job vacancy?"

I held my breath as I grinned, probably showing too much teeth, but since I still wasn't one hundred percent sure how I planned to work in Norway, I needed to try. While the guys didn't seem put-out to be hosting me, it would be nice to have a job to help put bread and butter on the table, and maybe save up for a new camera.

Oddvar let out a deep and long sigh, his wispy eyebrows twitching on a phantom wind, as he narrowed his eyes at me. He crossed his arms, and the material of his sweater, the color of which matched his gray hair, bunched around his elbows. "You know how to use a coffee machine?" he asked in his heavily accented and slightly mismatched English.

"Sure." Put hot water in a container, let steep, add accoutrement. Pretty simple.

He pointed to the fancy Italian espresso machine with all the shiny knobs and dials, including a milk frothing wand. "Do you know how to use *that*?"

I pursed my lips. Admittedly, he had me there. I was more of a stop at Starbies or Dunks (depending on what state I was in) kind of gal, but I could always learn. And the café seemed like the best fit for me out of all the businesses in town.

"No, but I'm sure I could find a good teacher around here," I replied, giving him an obnoxiously obvious wink followed by my brightest smile. The same smile I'd used with my mother any time I got in trouble growing up. "And I make a mean sandwich."

He huffed through his nose like a bull, the corners of his mouth remaining in a straight line. "I will think about it." He turned his back on me and started washing something in the sink.

Taking his words as a dismissal, I turned back to the room, refusing to abandon hope. It wasn't an outright no.

Espen still wasn't here, so I sat at one of the vacant tables and perused the little menu that I'd already memorized.

"Sorry I'm late," Espen said as he planted a kiss on my cheek a few minutes later, a chilly breeze following him in through the door. "Neighboring police station called and had some questions."

My smile faltered and a lump grew in my throat, thinking back on all of the drama that had happened earlier this fall. "Is everything all right?"

"Absolutely perfect. They just wanted to review some logistics to prep for next year's tourist season." He briefly glanced over his shoulder to the counter, and my nerves eased. "Have you ordered yet?"

I shook my head.

"How about a quick sandwich here and then coffee to-go?"

"Sounds perfect. Goat cheese with jam, please." I'd become addicted to the brown-colored goat cheese, caramelized whey tasting both sweet and salty at the same time. Paired with some nice bread and a dollop of strawberry jam, the simple dish was heaven for the tastebuds. For some reason, it reminded me of peanut butter and jelly sandwiches.

"Whatever you want, Lennie." Espen smiled.

Now, that was one of my favorite sentences.

After we'd finished our lunch, we grabbed our to-go coffee and sauntered up the hillside toward Espen's little cabin. He still lived here, but it was significantly smaller than Øyvin's boathouse, so it had become more of a little getaway space for us. Most nights Espen joined us at Øyvin's, unless he was working a late shift and didn't want to wake us up. How we'd fallen into such an easy living situation, I wasn't quite sure. But it likely had something to do with their protective instincts... and as I was still jobless, I wasn't going to say no to free rent. Not in this economy.

The area near the cabin was a grassy field with tufts of bushes and random boulders that looked like a Norse god had errantly chucked onto the landscape like salt crystals. The forest at our backs was still green thanks to the plethora of evergreens, but a few spindly and bare trunks dotted the treeline. I clutched my coffee cup to my chest, relishing in the warmth seeping into my hands and the steam brushing across my chin. The temperature had dropped overnight, and I'd overheard rumblings at the café that snow was on the way. Just the thought of seeing the village blanketed in a layer of snow had me giddy with excitement. Paired with this picturesque scenery of the mountains rising high around the edges of the fjord, Skolvik was bound to look like a snowglobe.

"This seems like a good spot to practice," Espen said, bursting my thought bubble. He bent down to set his coffee cup on a wooden table outside his cabin. Each of the four stools surrounding it were stumps and the table itself was the center beam of a larger log, befitting the Forest Fae.

I let out an exasperated sigh and took a swig of my coffee for moral support, needing more caffeine in my system. Using the magical energy wasn't physically draining, at least not to the extent that *I* was using the magic, but training with the guys was mentally exhausting.

"You ready?" Espen asked, rolling his shoulders like he was about to spar with me in a ring.

I set my coffee beside his and pulled off my hat, tucking it away in my jacket pocket. "Could I interest you in a quick *yoga* session instead?" It was part-joke, part-serious, refusing to admit nervous energy was eating away at my stomach with each failed attempt. I only had a few days left to master this skill if Espen's Christmas Eve plans were to be fulfilled, and I didn't want to let him down.

Espen flicked his thick brows, eyes roving over my body and leaving a heated trail behind. "Tempting, tempting, but we need to do this. The sooner you learn how to shield your ears, the better."

I huffed, but couldn't disagree.

He stepped forward and placed his hand on my left shoulder, dropping the mirage he'd magicked over my ears this morning before he left for work. "Now, stand over there"—he pointed to the field where we'd once done some very enjoyable *yoga* underneath the night sky and aurora borealis—"and let's use yesterday's lesson with Øyvin as a starting point."

I let out a deep breath and wandered into the field before turning on my heel to face him.

He nodded for me to proceed, watching me closely like I was a student or one of his Forest Fae soldiers.

I closed my eyes and focused on the mental picture I'd conjured up of my human ears like Øyvin had instructed yesterday. Pulling on the energy in my sternum, I placed my hand on my shoulder and dragged a piece of it up toward my ears, imagining it curling up my spine and depositing it at my ears.

"Well done," Espen exclaimed, and I fluttered my eyes open.

He was beaming, and the sight made my heart pitter-patter.

"Now, let's see how long you can hold it for." My stomach sank at his words, but he was right. I needed to be able to hold the magical mirage for hours on end without giving it much thought. "Ask me a question."

"How long did it take you to learn how to do this?" I asked, waving my hand at my head.

He leaned back against the table edge and crossed his ankles. "To hold it consistently? A couple of years. To hold it for a few hours at a time?" He tilted his head from one side to the other. "Maybe a few weeks."

I shifted on my feet and shoved my hands in my jacket pockets, hiding them from the cold air. "How old were you then?"

He took a deep breath and wiped his hand across his forehead, pushing aside his dark floppy hair. "About five years old."

I groaned. Yeah, this really was the basic of basics in the magic fae world.

"Don't worry," he said. "You'll get there quickly. I don't doubt it for a second. And look, you've been able to hold it while we've been talking without any flickering."

My ears did indeed still feel a little warmer than usual—maybe only by a degree or two, but it was noticeable. I took another deep breath and let it out through my mouth, watching as it fogged in the cool air.

"Keep asking me questions. Let's see if you can hold it until I have to go back to work."

"You mean keep distracting myself?"

He nodded.

I brushed an errant hair away from my face. "What do you normally do during the festive season? Do you stay in Skolvik or…?"

A soft, happy look crossed Espen's face and his amber eyes warmed. "It depends. Sometimes I take the Christmas shifts so my colleagues can enjoy the festivities with their families, and other times I head north to visit my sisters and my nieces and nephew."

"What was your original plan for this year? Before I showed up?"

He tilted his head and assessed me, before pushing off the table and taking a few steps closer. "I was going up north to see them."

My heart stuttered and my eyes widened, guilt seeping in. "I took you away from your family?"

Espen shook his head gently. "It's all right. I *want* to be here with you. I've had countless Christmasses with them and will have hundreds more. I'll video call them. Ingrid and Turi have already scheduled a time."

My shoulders dropped and I let out a small sigh of relief. If there was one thing in this world that I could classify as the most important thing in my life, it would be my family. No matter how far removed I was from them, I'd be lost without them—even my Mom and her incessant worry for me and interest in getting me married off. Part of me was a little sad that I was missing Christmas with them—the food, hanging up all the lights with Dad, and watching my nieces tear into their presents early in the morning while the rest of us adults chugged coffee to wake up. The other part of me was excited to experience my first Norwegian Christmas and make new traditions, new memories.

Espen took a few steps closer, his smile never faltering, and my heart did that weird fluttering thing it had been doing lately. I continuously ignored it whenever I was in his or Øyvin's presence, even if it had been happening more often over the last few weeks.

"Well, I'm glad I'll get to spend the day with—"

"Night," he interjected. "We celebrate on Christmas Eve."

"Night, right." I mumbled as he took another step closer, like a predator homing in on his prey. A pleasant shudder ran through me, but I shook it off. "I'm glad I'll get to spend the *night* with you."

A sly grin spread on his lips and my mind drifted to *other* nighttime activities, warmth drifting down and settling low in my abdomen. *Perhaps I should get Espen a Kama Sutra book for Christmas. Win, win.*

Espen's eyes dipped from mine and landed on my chest. He swept his tongue across his bottom lip before his gaze leisurely drifted back up to mine. He took a few steps closer, bringing us almost toe to toe.

"What?" I asked, my voice more breathy than I'd intended as I studied his expression.

He looked down and back up again, his eyes turning molten, and I glanced down.

For fuck's sake.

"How long?" I asked with a shake of my head, peering back up at Espen.

His grin turned wicked.

"How long have my tits been out, Espen?" Because sure enough, at some point during our conversation I must have accidentally magicked myself half-naked thanks to my R-rated wandering mind. My jeans were still on, but from my shoulders down to my hips, I appeared stark naked. Thankfully, it was a weak mirage and I actually had my jacket on so I wasn't cold or nipping hardcore. But, still...

Espen let out a throaty chuckle and leaned in. "Not too long." He trailed his fingers up both of my arms, leaving goosebumps in his wake. "Did you get distracted?"

"Maybe." Yes. Definitely. 100 percent. Dammit.

He tucked a lock of my hair behind my ear and dipped his head, brushing his lips across my cheek, then down my neck. "If I didn't have to go back to work," he whispered, sending tingles down my spine as his words caressed my skin.

"What would you do?"

He swallowed hard and let out an audible groan. "I'd treat these with the care and attention they deserve."

I tilted my head, breathing in his smell of moss and leather. He rested his hands on my shoulders, then slowly swept them down—

Beep, beep, beep.

He let out a dissatisfied grunt and stepped back, pulling his phone out of his jacket pocket. "Duty calls."

An annoyed sound escaped from my throat as I shook off the heady sensation coursing through my veins.

He turned off his phone alarm and sauntered back to the table, picking up our coffees. "Well, this has been good progress. You held your ears there for roughly twenty minutes. I dare say, if you focus, you may be able to hold it for a couple of hours when we go to the caroling festivities on Christmas Eve."

He handed me my drink, and I took a sip of the coffee and straightened up. *I could definitely do that.* I just needed not to think about getting naked, or the guys getting naked, or *yoga.*

Espen sauntered back down the hillside toward the woods that separated his cabin from the village.

"Ummm, Espen."

"Yeees?" He turned and gave me a sly grin.

"Are you forgetting something?" I motioned to my boobs which were still on display.

He took a sip of his drink and tilted his head. "I don't think so."

"Espen Solbakke..."

"Okay, okay, okay." He traipsed back up to me and placed his hand on my shoulder. A moment later my nudity mirage was gone, replaced by the clothes I was actually wearing. He turned and took two steps before he said over his shoulder, "You should try that trick again later, though."

I narrowed my eyes at him. "Only if you're a good boy and eat your veggies at dinner."

"I'm always a good boy." He winked and gave me his signature sunny grin.

I chuckled and swatted his ass. Together we walked back into the village—him breaking off to head back to the police station, and me back to the boathouse to continue practicing.

5

LENNIE

Tonight was the night: Little Christmas Eve, as they called it in Norway. The day before Christmas Eve, which I couldn't help thinking of as Christmas Eve Eve.

After my training session with Espen yesterday lunchtime, I'd spent the rest of the afternoon and this morning practicing holding the ear mirage at the boathouse in front of a mirror. Slowly but surely, I'd increased my total time. The guys had encouraged me to get my time above an hour and, so far, I'd been able to hit that, but not longer.

Tonight, the guys set a new challenge—Espen would drop his magic over my ears, then I would need to pull it back in place and walk through town without anyone noticing. The guys would meet me back at home.

Nervous energy threatened to distract my shaky hold on my magic since I still hadn't quite mastered using it, but it was nearly midnight. The only thing wending its way through the village was a cold breeze that nipped at my nose and cheeks, so, if I failed, the odds of me running into a human were pretty slim.

My breath fogged in the air as I tightened the scarf around my neck and removed my scarlet-and-gray hat, stuffing it into my jacket pocket. The fjord lapped gently against the rocks beside us on the north side of town, near the path that led to Solveig's house. Diffused moonlight shone down on the landscape, painting everything in a soft glow, and all of the plant life was fully entrenched in its winter slumber.

Espen set his hands on my shoulders and turned me to face him. "Are you ready?"

"You tell me, Coach."

Øyvin snorted as he watched our exchange with his arms crossed.

"You're going to do great." Espen swept his arms down my own, my jacket rustling from his touch. He placed my hands in his before adding, "I know you can do this. I believe in you."

I couldn't help the pitter-patter of my heart at the sentiment, hearing the warmth in his words. If this were a romantic comedy movie, this would be when I swooned and hearts would flutter around me like butterflies. But, instead I was in Norway, about to test run my newly acquired magic in a public space for the first time.

"I commend your positivity," I replied, squeezing his hands, wanting to believe him.

"Just don't fuck up," Øyvin added with a shit-eating grin that I wanted to wipe off his face.

Yeah, that look triggered some of the Martin Family competitiveness, and, knowing him, he'd said it for that exact purpose. "Is that a challenge, Asshole?"

Espen stepped between us, blocking my view of the Fjord Fae and his now surly expression. "I'll drop the current mirage and we'll leave you here. Ready?"

I nodded and straightened up, determination overtaking the last of my nerves. It was go-time.

Espen placed his palm against my left shoulder and let out a long, steady breath before removing his hand. A tiny wave of warmth swept over the sides of my head, and I instinctively reached up, feeling the sensitive points. *Still so bizarre.* I'd probably never get over the fact that I'd been born human, but was now part fae, too. Thanks, Halvar.

Espen planted a swift kiss to my cheek, before he headed into town. Øyvin playfully pinched my ass as he sauntered past with a smirk. He clearly didn't believe I could do this, but damn did that spur me on to prove him wrong.

With the two of them strolling into the village and out of sight, I was alone. Just me, the cool wind, a frosty smell, and my very fae features.

I shook off any lingering doubts and paced in a quick circle, focusing my thoughts and energy. I could do this. I'd done it for the last few days, and it was magic that was easily used by all the fae—an evolutionary tactic they'd been using for centuries to stay hidden among the humans. If all of the fae before me could do it, then dammit, so could I, even if I was a brand new demi-fae.

I took a deep breath and placed my right hand on my left shoulder, right above the end of the lightning-shaped scar that ran up the entirety of my arm—the one that had been left behind when Halvar transferred magic into me as Queen Freija died.

Closing my eyes, I focused on picturing my ears as they'd once been; rounded, human, normal. With the image firmly in mind, I pulled at the well of power within me, dragging it up my neck and leaving some at my ears. Warmth tingled under my skin, the tell-tale sign I was doing it. I was actually doing it. *I can do this!*

I shimmied with excitement, thoughts of how I'd make Øyvin repay me for his snarky comments later tonight filling my head. A wash of warmth swept down me, like the magic was whooshing back into place but missed its mark and hit my toes. I leaned over and glanced into the fjord to my right, checking my appearance on the water's surface, and brushed my fingers across my ears. Still pointy. Damn. Then I peered down.

"Shit."

From my collarbones down to my pinky toes, I was as naked as the day I was born. Or at least, it looked that way. I knew it was just a strong, physical mirage, but no one else would know that. If I stumbled across someone, they'd see me ready for the Polar Bear Plunge in my birthday suit.

I scuttled behind a nearby (thankfully empty) trashcan, ducking down to curl my body over itself before any late night walkers spotted me. I could triage this situation. Unfortunately, my magic hadn't ever stayed in place long enough for me to practice undoing it, so I had no idea what to do. Fuck me sideways, why was nothing ever easy?

Assuming undoing magic was the same as engaging it, I let my mind dial in on the clothes I'd been wearing—was technically *still* wearing beneath my accidental exposure—and closed my eyes. Feeling the warmth of my power in my sternum swirling around, I drew on some and tried to pull it across my body, like drawing the blinds shut or pulling a blanket over myself. My skin tingled and the wind nipped at my cheeks, but I held my concentration until I estimated enough time had passed. Opening my eyes to the fog of my own breath, I peeked down and...

I was still butt naked.

Fantastic.

The guys were going to laugh themselves to death when I walked through the door looking like this. I could picture it now, Espen curled up on the floor gasping for breath, while Øyvin leaned against the kitchen counter trying to hide his laughs behind his hand.

Brushing my free hand across my other arm, I shuddered at the weird sensation of feeling skin against skin, my mind battling with the conflicting senses. No goosebumps formed and my arm hairs didn't stand on end in the cold December air since I technically still had my jacket and pants on, but it *felt* like my skin to my touch. And yet, everything was visible, from my tits and bits, to the gnarly lightning-shaped scar that ran the length of my left arm. *Can't I go five minutes without landing myself in a chaotic situation?*

I looked around, wondering what else I could do. There was a wooden bench to my left, a metal bicycle rack on the other side of the path, and a signboard a few paces away with notices about tomorrow night's caroling event plastered all over it. Lights were off in the few light-colored buildings that marked the start of town, the small shops having closed for the day hours ago. There wasn't anything to save me.

I was going to have to streak.

With a sigh, I straightened up from my hiding spot and ran.

6

LENNIE

My arms pumped at my sides and my legs moved faster than ever before as I bolted into the downtown core of the village. The clouds hung heavy in the fjord, the smell of imminent snow lingered in the air, and almost all the houses and storefronts had turned their lights off as we closed in on midnight. I was a veritable Cinderella. Only, in my case, I'd lost a whole lot more than a shoe.

I wound around the corner, past the large, twinkling town Christmas tree, and sprinted into the village square by the harbor front. Strings of lights surrounded the cobble-stoned area, wreaths of greenery hung on lampposts lending a faint smell of pine to the air, and a band-stand was half-erected beside the obnoxiously large evergreen. If I had a spare moment to admire it all, I would, but as it were...

The lights suddenly turned off at Fisken, the local restaurant that looked out onto the square and harbor. The front door swung open and I immediately ducked behind a large, boxlike cement planter with a skinny tree in the middle. Crouching and panting heavily, I watched as Solveig and her two friends, Jorunn and Dagny—the old ladies I'd volunteered with to clean up after the landslides this past autumn—stepped out of the establishment arm-in-arm. Their broad smiles and bubbling laughter had my stomach sinking to my toes. Shit. Had they seen me?

Solveig did a stutter step between her friends, which had them teetering and sent them into further fits of giggles. I relaxed my shoulders and bit my lip, unable to fight the grin though. The three friends were tipsy, chattering away in Norwegian. Thankfully, the magic trick that Nora had pulled on me earlier this year still worked, so I understood everything they said.

"Watch out for the lamppost," Solveig snickered, shifting her white-haired friend out of the way at the last second. Dagny bowed her head to the street light in apology, then grabbed the hem of her long puffer-jacket and curtseyed.

"We shall have to dance another time. The aquavit has given me two left feet," she muttered to the lamppost, then spun to her friends with a wobble. "I wouldn't mind a dance with that Øyvin, though. So handsome. So dreamy."

I scoffed a laugh that came out a little louder than expected. All three of them whipped their heads in my direction and I ducked, hoping they hadn't spotted me. My heart pounded against my ribs and my hands started to feel clammy. *Shit, shit, shit, shit, shit.* I was going to end up naked at the police station where all of Espen's colleagues would see me, including his boss. I would be the talk of the town... *again.*

"Did you see that?" one of them said.

A loud hiccup echoed through the empty town square. "I saw you drink your weight in aquavit, that's what I saw."

"Are you sure your bifocals are working, dear?"

"My eyesight is perfectly fine, Solveig. Perhaps it was a *nisse.*"

I frowned, trying to remember the story Espen had told me last week. *Nisse* were elf-like creatures from Norwegian folktales that lived on farms and helped take care of the animals. On Christmas Eve the farmers would set out a rice pudding called *grøt*, which he'd described to be like oatmeal with cinnamon and sugar on it, plus a small square of butter. Did the tipsy trio really believe in *nisse*? Or maybe, just maybe, the tales about *nisse* were really stories about the fae who took care of the environment, including the animals?

"It *is* almost Christmas Eve, perhaps a *nisse* wandered down from the Langholm farm for a swim?" Solveig said.

Another hiccup. "I could do with a swim right about now."

"Oh no, you don't." Scuffeling and grunting sounded, and I peeked around the corner to watch them yank their friend away from the harbor. I mean, I couldn't blame her for wanting a dip after drinking aquavit—that stuff was pure fire—but it *was* the middle of December and the fjord was freezing cold. Unfortunately, I knew this firsthand since I'd taken an unscheduled plunge last week after asking Øyvin to pull the stick out of his ass.

I stayed hunched over, leaning against the cement planter, and waited for their chatter to die off as they sauntered home through the village. After several minutes of silence and no other sightings of humans, I rose and ran.

My lungs heaved, and I cursed myself for this unplanned cardio, especially in the middle of the night. Why, of all the times I'd tried to use my magic, did it decide that *now* was the right time for it to work properly and stay firmly in place? *Figures.*

Skolvik at night glowed under the dim beams of its street lights in a blur of festive reds, whites, and greens as I streaked through town. Reaching a turn in the road, I leaned against the building beside me and peered around the corner to make sure the coast was clear. The street was empty, the glow from storefronts' night lights the only thing in the roadway. A skittering noise sounded back the way I'd come from, but I didn't see anyone. *Probably just a cat.* With a deep breath, I pushed off the wall and bolted up the main street, hoping none of the stores had security cameras—and, if they did, that I was fast enough to be considered a ghost.

I pushed one foot in front of the other, my breaths sawing in and out of my lungs, cold air nipping at my face. Two short blocks to go and I would be on the road toward Øyvin's house with minimal street lamps and enough darkness to hide my nu—

An arm reached out from the side street to my left, and yanked me aside. It all happened so fast I didn't have time to scream or yelp or piss my invisible pants.

I grappled with my captor, but was spun around and landed with a *thud* against the wood wall of the white building. My assailant lightly pressed their forearm against my collarbone, both of my wrists ensnared and held above my head.

I glanced up into a pair of blue eyes full of glee.

"Hello, Trouble."

7

LENNIE

Before I could thrash out of his hold, Øyvin removed his forearm from my collarbone and tilted my chin up with his finger and thumb. He gave me a smug lopsided grin and swept his tongue across his bottom lip as he surveyed my state of undress.

"I had a feeling things would take a turn," he said, a large dollop of victory lacing his tone. "You have an uncanny ability to land yourself in troublesome situations."

"Good thing my middle name is Trouble, then, isn't it?" I goaded him, wholly unwilling to address the elephant in the room, so to speak. *Tatas who? Never heard of them.*

He stepped forward and pressed his body into mine as he squeezed my wrists pinned above my head, a reminder of who was in control. I sucked in a breath and swallowed hard, the tension between us pulsing. My nerve-endings sparked from the streaking adrenaline, plus having Øyvin so near, and my head filled with the lusty haze that always seeped in whenever he stood this close to me.

Øyvin's gaze dipped to my mouth and his palm rested on the side of my neck as he brushed his thumb across my bottom lip. It took every ounce of self-control I had to not press my tongue to the tip.

He shifted, his muscles taught, jaw tight as he gave me more of his weight. Every time we were alone together I wanted to push his buttons, see how grumbly he could *really* get, and then climb him like a tree. It was that never-ending fire again—flitting from inferno one minute to soft embers the next.

Before I lost all sense of composure, I cleared my throat. "Where's Espen? Has he been hiding along the route back to the boathouse waiting to jump scare me, too?" He definitely wouldn't do that; Espen was too kind, but I wouldn't put it past him to take up position and watch the events unfold.

"He had faith in your ability." Øyvin let out a mocking snort.

I scowled. "And you didn't?"

"I most certainly did not."

"Ye of little faith."

"I trust that you'll get into trouble whenever an opportunity presents itself." He pushed his hips into mine, and I returned the favor rolling my lower abdomen across him, heat spiraling up through me. His length pressed against me, and my breaths came harder, my core reacting to him. Needing him. *So much for that composure.*

"Espen's at home?" My words came out breathy and wanton, a clear signal that my head was taking a nap and my hormones were now in the driver's seat.

"He's waiting there ready to give you your reward."

"A reward?" I asked, wiggling my hands to signal I needed him to release them from where he had them pinned above my head or I'd lose all feeling in them.

He immediately dropped my wrists, but shifted his free hand to my hip and continued holding me firmly in place. "You shouldn't get anything for this disaster of a test." He tilted his head back toward the part of town I'd just run through.

"What? You don't think successfully streaking through the village deserves a reward?"

He let out an exasperated groan and, before I could make a move, pulled us away from the wall and hoisted me over his broad shoulder, my butt pointing toward the sky.

"You most definitely do *not* deserve a *reward*."

I squeezed my thighs together, but was pretty sure I was now more exposed than ever. "But you're going to give me one anyway?"

That earned me a smack to the ass.

"You're not even going to fix my nudity?" I asked.

"I don't mind the consequences of your actions," he grumbled. "In fact, I prefer you like this."

"At your mercy?"

"Exactly."

Øyvin set me down outside the boathouse's front door and pushed it open, corralling me through.

"How'd you do?" Espen asked as we strolled inside, the lingering smell of linen and pine making it feel homey here. Since Øyvin hadn't bothered to help me with my state of undress, Espen's eyes bugged out when he spotted me in my birthday suit. "What happened?"

I placed my hands on my hips and beamed victoriously, done attempting to cover up. "I successfully streaked across the village." Focus on the positives, right? I could practically *feel* Øyvin's eye roll behind me as he pulled off his boots and set them neatly on the shoe rack by the door. "I'm here to collect my reward."

Yeah, I was pushing it, but don't blame a girl for trying.

"She thinks she deserves a reward for failure," Øyvin huffed as he sauntered past me into the kitchen. He leaned against the clean and tidy kitchen counter, a partially amused look spread across his face.

"Failure is in the eye of the beholder," I retorted, tipping my chin up.

Espen chuckled and drew my attention as he slowly stepped closer. His gaze roved over me from my toes to the tips of my ears, heat flaring in his eyes.

"Did anyone see you?" he asked, briefly looking toward Øyvin before turning his focus to me.

I shook my head. The only person that had spotted me was in the room with us and not a threat. Well, at least not to *us*. I'd seen what Øyvin could do on the battlefield—hell, I'd even witnessed him try to drown people on the spot—but I doubted he'd ever pull any of those tactics on me... unless I tried commandeering his boat again.

Espen stepped in front of me, eyes brimming with heat. Before I could utter anything, he placed his hand on my left shoulder and I felt the magic shift through me, removing the naked mirage. My clothes were back where they belonged and where they'd been hiding underneath the magic.

A slow smile swept across Espen's face and I squirmed under his heady stare. "You want a reward?"

I nodded and shifted my weight to one side, popping my hip.

His smile grew bigger and my pulse started humming faster. "Well then. We'll have to play a game and see if you win."

That stubborn competitive switch turned on in my brain once more. "A game?" I asked, my voice sounding all coy.

Espen brushed his hand across his beard and winked. "A game."

"What are the rules?"

"We make the rules," Øyvin said from the kitchen, and the low tone of his voice sent a shiver down my spine that landed at my core.

A look passed between the two fae before Espen turned back to me and beamed. I got the feeling I'd be both winning and losing this game. "Go on then, what's round one?"

Espen grabbed hold of the zipper on my jacket and stared into my eyes. I swallowed hard as he spoke. "Did you run past Fjordland Gullsmed?"

The silversmith-slash-jewelry-store was one of the first buildings I'd passed on my mad naked dash, but it was closed, like all the other stores in the village. I nodded.

He yanked down my zipper and I let out a guffaw as he pushed my jacket off my shoulders and arms before throwing it over the back of the sofa.

"They have a security camera on the corner of the shop," he said, and my stomach sank. *Shit.* I'd hoped that the locals didn't have heightened security on their buildings, but I should have guessed a jeweler might secure his wares. The store owner was going to have a nice video of my tits and bits on his camera footage.

"Did you run past the toy store?"

I scoffed. Of course I had, it was two doors—*Oh no*. My breath hitched as it dawned on me. Another camera. Espen's lip twitched. "They have a camera, too?" I asked.

He nodded and grabbed the hem of my sweater, then unceremoniously pulled it up and over my head before throwing it aside.

Øyvin snickered, and I gave him the middle finger. I could think of worse games than strip whatever-this-was, even if I was about to lose terribly. Maybe winning would come after I was naked?

"How about the library?"

I sighed. "Yes, I ran past *biblioteket*," I said, trying out the word I'd recently learned in Norwegian. I'd probably butchered it, but now was not the time for lessons—at least not that kind. "Let me guess. They have a handy-dandy camera, too?"

Espen nodded again and then tackled the long-sleeved t-shirt under my sweater. As soon as that landed beside the kitchen table, he leaned in and swept one hand around my back. Before I could ascertain what he was doing, the clasp on my bra sprung free and it fell down my arms. I shook it off and cast it aside, wholly impressed by his skill.

I arched a brow as I stared up into Espen's amber eyes that had gone molten at the sight of me half-dressed in the middle of the living room. "They have two cameras?"

"Mm-hmm."

This was torture. I wanted to lean in and return the favor, but as I lifted my hands to do just that, Espen tutted and gently tapped them away. "Hands down. No touching."

I clenched my fists and rolled my shoulders as heat swirled in my core, my nipples hardening in the cool air.

"Get on with it," Øyvin grumbled and I chanced a look at him. The blue in his eyes had darkened and his knuckles were white where he gripped the counter behind him. He was as tortured as I was. Good.

Espen knelt down and started unlacing my shoes.

"What are those for?" I asked, wondering what other cameras I'd accidentally mooned tonight.

"Speed," he practically choked out and I was glad I wasn't the only one overwhelmed by the heady tension in the room. My nerves tingled in anticipation, and it took every ounce of effort I had to maintain any sense of composure, let alone ability to keep my hands off him. When he finished with the laces, he helped me out of my shoes, then immediately unbuttoned and pulled down the zipper on my jeans.

"Hey!"

Espen grinned and peered up at me through his lashes, and I almost melted from that one look alone. Achingly slowly, he brushed his hands up my calves, thighs, and stopped at my hips right at the waist of my pants. I sucked in a breath and waited for his next move, desperate to rake my hands through that floppy hair of his, to hold him to the spot that desperately wanted attention.

"Did you run past the Christmas tree by the harbor?"

"She did," Øyvin grumbled before I could confirm that I had indeed run through the town square by the waterfront.

Cold air bit at me as Espen yanked down my jeans and underwear in one swift move. I let out a whimper, my core needing this to move along quicker, my desire to have this man inside me unfurling through every limb. "Are there security cameras to guard the tree?"

Espen let out a throaty chuckle and rose to his feet, skimming his hands up my thighs, waist, then sides as he stood. "No." His reply came out on a shuddered breath. "There's a web-cam that live streams the harbor to the town website."

Fuck me.

"Why did you even have me try the ears thing and walk through town knowing there were so many cameras?" I reached for Espen's chest, but he grabbed my wrists and held them in the space between us.

"It's one thing to explain away the ears as a *nisse* costume. It's a whole other thing to explain public nudity," he said.

"What if someone spotted Øyvin carrying me home?" I challenged.

"*She had too much aquavit and lost her clothes,*" Øyvin said, pretending to give a hypothetical excuse to some poor witness.

Okay, that was a viable explanation considering the potency of the beverage and the effect it had on me, aside from making me feel like a fire breathing dragon.

"We may have to increase her magic lessons," Øyvin said as he sauntered over, opening and closing his fists. "If she's to master the basics—"

"Oh, I agree," Espen interjected, narrowing his eyes at me, and my stomach flip-flopped at the rolling tone in his voice. "But will she be a good student?"

"Unlikely," Øyvin muttered, his finger tracing across my pointed ear and down the side of my neck.

I squirmed, my heart hammering in my chest as a desperate desire for both of them took over. "Teach me a lesson, then."

Espen dropped to his knees and Øyvin came up behind me.

Not holding back, Espen didn't tease me anymore, grabbing my thigh and lifting it to his shoulder as he swept his tongue over my center, while Øyvin pushed my hair aside and kissed up the side of my neck. Unable to restrain myself any longer, I plunged my fingers into Espen's hair and held him where I needed him. He obliged by grazing his teeth across my sensitive clit and sent shocks of pleasure through me.

Øyvin swept his hands across my front and palmed one breast in each hand, gently kneading them. The pull and pressure from him was enough to have me panting already, moaning for more.

I lifted my arms and entwined my hands behind Øyvin's neck, pressing my breasts more firmly into his palms. He teased and tugged at my nipples until they hardened, sending bliss through my veins. The feel of his hands sweeping across my skin had me writhing against his body, his cock pressing against my rear.

I gasped as Espen pressed a finger to my opening, drawing lazy circles around my entrance. My knees buckled and Øyvin wrapped a muscled arm around my middle, holding me upright. As Espen pushed his finger inside me, I let out an agonized moan, my head falling back against Øyvin's chest from the waves of pleasure.

I wasn't going to last much longer at this rate. They knew every button to press, every part of me that was currently walking a tightrope awaiting the crash into oblivion. They were the puppet masters and I was theirs to wield—and damn, did I love it.

Espen picked up the pace, adding a second finger to his ministrations and I let out an undignified noise. A second later, with Øyvin's lips on my neck and Espen's tongue swirling around my clit, I shattered.

My breaths came in shuddered pants, my entire body convulsing through the bliss. A pleasurable feeling I never wanted to end.

Espen shot up to his feet and pressed his lips to mine, and I tasted myself on him. Øyvin didn't back away, leaving me sandwiched between the two fae, heat and hedonism filling the air around us.

"Well, that was…" I couldn't even finish the sentence. Words and breath evaded me.

Øyvin wrapped his arms around my middle while Espen swiped his thumb across my mouth. "Let's take this upstairs," Espen murmured, tilting my head so our eyes met. The passion and need in his eyes sent another tingling sensation down my legs and I was glad Øyvin still held me upright.

"Yes, please," I responded, my voice barely a whisper.

"I love it when you're polite," Øyvin mocked, his smile pressing against my shoulder.

"Do more of that and I'll not only be polite, I'll start begging."

"Perfect."

8

LENNIE

Øyvin deposited me on his bed, the white sheets soft and cool beneath my heated body. "Lie down," he murmured, and I did as requested, my eyes never drifting from his. He reached behind his head and, in one swift move, pulled off his cream-knit sweater, leaving his torso bare. Out of the corner of my eye, I caught Espen doing the same, dropping his shirt on the floorboards.

Before I could say anything, Øyvin wrapped his hands around my thighs and pulled me to the edge of the bed, lining me up perfectly with the seam of his jeans. Meanwhile, Espen climbed up on the bed beside me, kneeling near my head.

Øyvin unzipped his jeans and pulled out his cock, the length hard and ready. My heart raced as a condom packet flew over me and landed at the edge of the bed. Øyvin nodded to Espen, and I looked back to find the Forest Fae returning the nod. Somehow the two of them were on the same wavelength and, with my toes curling and core already dripping in anticipation, I wanted in on whatever they were planning to do to me, as soon as possible.

Øyvin rolled on the condom and notched himself at my entrance. Slowly, inch by teasing inch, he entered me. My breath caught as I squirmed with each tiny push, wanting and needing more, even as my core spasmed around him.

Once he'd fully settled inside me, Espen bent over me and took one of my nipples in his mouth, cupping my other breast with his warm hand. The feel of his tongue drawing circles around my peaked nipple had me losing all sense of composure, and I let out a throaty moan.

That was enough to get Øyvin moving, pulsing in and out of me in languid strokes. Together, the two of them worshiped my body. Espen explored every inch of my breasts with both his hands and his lips, while Øyvin worked me into a frenzy with each slow and unforgiving thrust. It didn't take long before my breaths shuddered and I gripped Espen's hair in both hands, holding onto him as my orgasm rocked through me, shattering every nerve ending in my body.

When I finally regained my breath, I mumbled, "Lesson learned," with a satisfied smile gracing my lips.

Both men chuckled, and the sound sent an eerie chill through my spine.

"Oh, Trouble," Øyvin said, pulling out and slamming back into me, my tender core clamping down around him once more. "We're just getting started."

Fuck.

9

LENNIE

The next morning, I'd just finished wrapping the guys' presents when a knock sounded at the bedroom door.

"All clear to enter?" Espen asked from the tiny hallway.

I frantically dove off the side of the bed and shoved the wrapped gifts under it, hiding them from view. "Come on in."

Espen opened the door and stuck his head around the corner, his dark-brown hair brushing across his forehead as I righted myself, sitting back on the bed. "Wow, you made a mess."

I scoffed and looked around at the parchment-style wrapping paper, some spools of red ribbon, and a single roll of green wrapping paper that I could only assume Espen had bought because it had trees on it. He wasn't entirely wrong about the mess, but this was tame compared to Martin Family Christmases, where my parents' bedroom was turned into 'Santa's workshop' for a day, and, one by one, we'd all take turns wrapping our gifts for one another. As the youngest, I was usually last and, by the time I got in there, it looked like drunken elves had run amok with sticky-bows, ribbon, and wrapping paper of all different colors.

This chaos was much more subdued.

"Did you need something?" I asked, nudging aside the parchment paper and watching it fall off the mattress with a thunk.

"I had an idea," Espen said, stepping into the room and closing the door behind him. His dark-green knit sweater hugged his shoulders and, for a split second, I wished he was wearing gray sweatpants instead of black jeans.

"What kind of idea?"

"Hiding your ears. I may have a different method that might be easier to conceptualize and hold for a longer period of time."

"Okay." I drew the word out hesitantly. "Proceed."

"We keep having you start your magic transition by touching your shoulder."

I nodded. "Yeah, because that's what you and all the other fae I've seen shift their appearance do."

"Right. But you don't *have* to do that."

"What?" I furrowed my brow as I crossed my arms, trying to follow his logic.

"We do that because that's how we were trained when we were little. Think of it as an ingrained motion or habit." He stepped across the room and sat down beside me, the bed shifting slightly under his weight. "You don't *have* to do that exact motion. In fact, to help you hold the mirage for longer, I want you to use a more specific movement."

My lips pursed, still not fully understanding what he wanted me to do instead.

"Instead of touching your shoulders, I want you to touch your earlobes when you try to shift the magic over your ears." He reached up and brushed his own thumbs and forefingers across his earlobes. "By doing that, you can focus or picture the magic going down your arms and directly into your ears instead of up and down your spine."

My mouth shifted into an *oh* expression. "I see where you're going with this. You want me to direct my magic away from my core to avoid any accidents of it 'falling' and taking my clothes with it."

He nodded. "That's a good way of thinking about it, yes. You want to give it a try?"

I mean, there was only one way to find out if it would work better than the shoulder method—not that said method hadn't been successful, but it hadn't been faultless either.

I shifted on the bed to face him, pulling my legs up underneath me.

"You have to want it," Espen coached, looking as hopeful as a puppy begging for a treat. "Truly focus on that image of human ears and *want* them to stay that way. Command the magic to stay there until you order it to relinquish its hold."

I took a deep breath and shut my eyes, shaking my arms at my sides in an attempt to get them and myself to relax and focus. "Think of it as putting on a hat," he added. "Keep the hat on until the end of the day."

"Or like earmuffs," I said, clenching my eyes shut and thinking about a set of fuzzy, pink earmuffs.

"Exactly."

Why hadn't I thought of this sooner? This was a much easier concept to grasp.

I closed my eyes and let my mind zero in on that thought, picturing my ears how they used to be as best as I could. With that image firmly in mind, I placed my hands on my earlobes and started pulling a tiny bit of my power from that well in my sternum, shifting it up my arms and onto my head as if I was putting on a pair of earmuffs I'd had as a child.

The heat tingled but settled nicely around my ears, warming them slightly.

"Well done," Espen said, and I opened my eyes to find him beaming at me.

"Now let's see how long I can hold it."

He patted my knee. "Come downstairs, fill in your immigration paperwork, and help me finish decorating the tree. Øyvin is working on tomorrow's dinner."

"Paperwork?" I knew I had adult shit to take care of, but in the past few days, that had completely slipped from my mind.

Espen nodded. "Yeah... uh. We need to have a conversation."

I followed Espen downstairs and he took a seat at the circular dining table, a stack of paper piled in front of him, while Øyvin chopped something at the kitchen counter.

"Are you ready to fill in your immigration documents?" Espen asked, a more serious tone in his voice and his usual smile missing.

"How bad can it be?" I countered, hoping this wouldn't take days or be too complex. I wanted to stay in the country, but also knew that immigration was a complicated matter. One that, in typical Lennie Martin fashion, I hadn't thought too much about when deciding to move here. "What do I need to do?"

The chopping stopped, and Espen straightened.

"Here's the thing." He patted the seat beside him and I took it, my stomach sinking lower and lower at the guys' hesitant expressions and actions. "You have two options really."

Øyvin coughed.

"Okay, you have one main option, but I want you to have a choice," Espen amended. My heart beat faster and I crossed my arms to steady myself, braced for whatever he was about to say. "Option one: you are a self-employed photographer that can prove an income of a certain, albeit quite significant, amount."

"Not an option," Øyvin grumbled from the kitchen counter, his back still turned to us, but clearly part of the conversation.

"Why is it not an option?" I challenged. It seemed quite reasonable to me. I mean, setting up a business wasn't easy and photography barely paid, but I could do family portraits and the like. The fact that my camera had been destroyed was certainly a problem I'd need to remedy in order to make it happen, but Øyvin's flat-out refusal to admit it was a possibility irked me.

Espen sighed and brushed his palm across his forehead, pushing his dark locks aside. "It's more of a challenge because the income level you have to prove is extremely high. If you don't meet it, you'll be forced to leave the country on very short notice."

I winced. Yeah, that didn't sound ideal. I'd hate to start feeling comfortable here only for the rug to be pulled out from underneath me. "What's option two?"

Øyvin set down his knife and turned, resting his lower back against the kitchen counter and crossing his arms. His eyes bore into mine and I shifted, clasping my hands together in my lap.

"What's option two, Espen?" I asked again, uneasiness settling in as I looked at the abnormally quiet and subdued Forest Fae.

"Option two is marriage."

I blinked twice.

My heart skipped three beats.

Did he just? No, I'm hallucinating. Too much sex would probably do that to a woman. Shattered nerve-endings and all that.

I glanced at Øyvin who didn't betray any emotion aside from his usual stoic grumpiness, then turned back to Espen and swallowed hard.

"Marriage?" I asked, my voice thick with a variety of emotions.

The word sounded foreign on my lips. I understood the *concept*, having watched two of my brothers tie the knot. But me?

Married?

I'd told my mother for years not to hold out hope and to quit asking when I'd be bringing a boy home for Thanksgiving. Then, this Autumn I'd brought home *two*, and they weren't exactly humans. Not that she knew that, but both her and Dad had liked them and thought they were very nice gentlemen. Everyone refrained from commenting on the fact that there were two though, which I appreciated considering we hadn't defined the relationship yet.

I wasn't ready, not then and not now.

Even after over a month together, I wasn't sure what *this* was entirely, other than that it made me happy. And that's what life was about right? Living in a way that made you happy and didn't cause harm to others.

Espen nodded slowly and scooted closer, taking my clammy hands in his as I looked back at him, eyes bugging like I'd seen a ghost. "Option two would see you marry me," he explained, his tone cool and calm in a way to encourage me to trust him. "I'd sponsor you as I have a human job that meets the income levels required by the Norwegian government. In order to make it legal, we'd have to have the signing or celebration within six months of approval."

Six months?

Six months from now it'd be June, and I still wouldn't have known these two an entire year. That seemed both outlandish, but also a little on-brand for me. Spontaneity was the name of the game.

I looked to Øyvin, who stood stock still, his gaze locked on me. "And you're okay with this arrangement?" I asked, not wanting him to feel left out. Was I even contemplating this?

"This is the only option that keeps you here long term, and I want you here," Øyvin replied, shoving his hands into the front pockets of his jeans that hung deliciously low on his hips. "However much trouble you cause."

A sharp, single syllable laugh escaped me, because, well, facts. Trouble seemed to find me 24/7. But my head and heart didn't miss those important four words in the middle. The stubborn and grumpy Fjord Fae had gone from hating my guts, to tolerating me, to wanting me here. I could pretend it was only to protect the fae secret, but his eyes betrayed a deeper emotion—one that sent warmth from the tips of my fingers to the ends of my toes. However much I annoyed the grouch—whether from purposefully putting things away in the wrong kitchen cabinet, or challenging him on the virtues of Beethoven—he cared about me, and I liked it.

"Øyvin suggested we hide you beneath the surface of the fjord," Espen continued, drawing my gaze away from the heat in Øyvin's. "But seeing as we don't know the full extent of your powers, but *do* know those powers came from the fjell and not the fjord, that didn't seem like a viable option. Plus, I'd like to follow the rules and give you an option to reject our proposal."

I stilled, because that's what this moment really was: a proposal. For immigration purposes, but it was still a proposal.

Did I want to marry him, though?

I'd be 29 this spring, which seemed an acceptable age to marry in my book. By Ohio standards that was practically ancient. In their eyes I was well on my way to spinster status and should've had three kids, a house, a poodle-mix, and a minivan with stick-figure family stickers on the back window announcing to the world how much procreating I'd done by now.

But I didn't live in Ohio anymore, nor did I want to return.

"If we do this"—I stood from my chair and rested my hands on the back, letting my eyes drift between the two of them—"I want it to be because we're trying to have me stay. I want this because it's for the safety of the fae secret and to help me better understand what the extent of my demi-fae powers are. If we decide this"—I waved my hand between the three of us, panic seizing me as I avoided the words *marriage* and *husband* like the plague—"whatever this is, isn't working even after we tie the knot, then I'm free to go."

That was the one thing I never wanted to give up: my own freedom. I'd been an independent person for so long. Doing what I wanted whenever I wanted to, and I enjoyed that lifestyle—the life I'd built for myself. But, then again, change wasn't always a bad thing.

I'd been through a literal and physical life change recently, one that would see my years extended for an unknown amount of time. Perhaps being a demi-fae could have me changing my preconceived plans? Maybe it already had?

"You will always be free to do whatever you want, Lennie," Espen said and Øyvin nodded in agreement. "We won't hold you here against your will."

"This doesn't mean we're *actually* defining the relationship," I said. A statement, not a question. "Only on paper."

I wasn't quite ready to make labels. It had only been a month or so. And while we'd decided not to sleep around or entertain anyone else, I didn't want to dive in head first; I wanted to slowly dip my toes and be happy, taking the days as they came.

"This is to keep you here legally." Espen nodded. "Nothing will change between us."

"Safer," Øyvin added. "You're right, it will keep you close to the fjell while we find out the extent of your powers and can keep you safe."

I bit my lip, refraining from remarking on his comment that 'I was right' which sounded like heaven to my ears. Instead, I took a deep breath and set my hands on my hips, trying to slow the galloping of my heart.

I was happy here.

I was building a new life for myself.

I had new powers that needed honing and protecting, and a local environment that needed that magic to help it thrive.

And I had two guys who cared about me. It was an unconventional situationship, but I liked what we had and if I didn't care about them, I wouldn't be here.

Fuck it. Fake marriage here I come.

"I'll go with option two, then."

Øyvin smirked, while Espen beamed and let out a massive sigh of relief, his head falling back briefly like he'd been holding his breath. Then he shifted out of his seat and got down on one knee. I sucked in a breath, my eyes widening at the sight.

"Lennie Martin of the humans and Fjell Fae, will you do me the honor of becoming my wife for immigration purposes, fae purposes, and for the sake of really good *yoga*?"

I snorted, but my lips curled into a smile. One couldn't not be happy around Espen.

"Espen Solbakke…" I paused and let him sweat a bit. "Yes."

Espen launched from his feet, picked me up and spun me around. Setting me back down, he planted a firm and passionate kiss against my lips that promised a celebratory *yoga* session. Before I lost my breath, he pulled back, grasped my shoulders and steered me to the mountain of documents on the kitchen table.

"Now, Ms. Martin who has been able to keep her ear magic up this entire conversation," he said, beaming from ear to ear. "Time to start signing these."

He landed a soft peck on my cheek, and my heart roared in triumph at holding the mirage the entire time, especially considering the distracting conversation, thoughts, and Espen's kisses. I didn't mind his little kisses, even when he did them in public. It was like he couldn't help himself, and just the thought of someone feeling that way about me, had my heart warming to temperatures I'd never felt before.

With the two fae watching on, I signed the paperwork.

10

ESPEN

She'd said yes.

My heart almost beat out of my chest when I'd suggested the idea of marriage knowing full well her feelings on *definitions*. But it was the only way to safely keep her in the country and close to Skolvik where we could help her and monitor her magic. As the first ever documented demi-fae, she was precious cargo.

Ultimately, she could always decide to go back to America. Even Halvar had given her that option this autumn. But if she chose to return to Ohio, we couldn't be there to help her should something go amok, which was bound to happen considering her proclivity for troublesome situations.

But, she'd said yes.

I stood in the kitchen after lunch with Lennie and Øyvin, helping with the prep-work for tonight's Christmas Eve dinner. Chopping away at the red cabbage, I couldn't stop myself from humming a happy little tune.

She'd said yes.

And I wasn't excluding Øyvin from this. He'd even agreed to it, without any counter-arguments or hesitation. Since the Norwegian government didn't have records of him, it had to be me. They *did* have me on record, albeit slightly modified to avoid any questions about my age, as I was employed by the local Police. Since I was a legal resident in human eyes, when Lennie eventually signed the marriage license, she could stay here legally and we could continue this thing the three of us had together.

She'd said yes, and I continued humming Christmas songs all afternoon, daydreaming about introducing her to my older sisters.

11

LENNIE

Bundled up to protect against the chilly weather—but sans hat so we could test my ability to keep my ears hidden—we sauntered into the village and headed toward the town square by the harbor I'd streaked through the night prior. Unlike last night, the entire esplanade was cordoned off tonight. Small tables were scattered around the space, covered in red and white tablecloths and booths lined the square, each one strung with twinkly lights. More people than I'd ever seen in Skolvik milled about under the night sky in their warmest jackets, crowding the sidewalks. The majority of folks had also donned red Santa hats with red tassels at the end, instead of white pom-poms that you'd see back in the US.

The smell of cocoa, pine, and a hint of smoke wafted through the air as we wandered past different booths, making our way toward the shimmering Christmas tree by the water where a small band was set up. The first booth we passed had men handing out flaming torches to adults and older children. I eyed the torches hesitantly, glancing around at the amount of wool people were wearing. Compared to the four-inch candles I was used to from Christmas Eve service in the US, this was a wild concept. It didn't escape my notice that neither of the guys offered me a torch, and I couldn't blame them—Trouble was my nickname, after all.

The scent of sugar and butter drew my attention to the second booth, eyeing the piles of several different types of cookies, none of which I recognized.

"Seven Types," Espen said, noting the platters and making a beeline for the table draped in red.

"What?" I asked, following and bumping into him as he came to a stop. Øyvin was thankfully paying more attention than me and didn't make this a sandwich situation by coming to a halt a few steps behind me. Ever since we'd reached the crowded street, he'd been on high alert, quietly peering over the masses, taking a few peeks at my ears, too. Probably making sure they hadn't accidentally turned pointy again.

"It's a Norwegian tradition," Espen said, drawing my focus back to the cookies that smelled so sweet, my mouth watered. "You make seven different varieties of cookies for Christmas."

"Only seven?" Don't get me wrong, that was a lot of cookies, but I'd grown up in a household with three older brothers who'd devoured anything and everything they could. Mom was constantly baking cookies over the holidays to accommodate our appetite for the sweet treats.

"Well, that's the thing." Espen perused the selection on the table that Solveig and her friends, Jorunn and Dagny, were manning. "There are no specifics around which seven to bake. So, each family has their own recipes and picks."

"And which is your favorite?" I asked, scoping out the platters on display, each with a little card at the front listing the name of the baked good.

Espen pointed to a golden, diamond-shaped one with crumbly bits of something on top. "Syrup snaps." The little sign beneath them said

Sirupsnipper. Not that I knew how to pronounce the word, but the part of my brain that cared about the Forest Fae decided to commit that little nugget to memory.

"How about yours, Øyvin? What's your poison?"

"Too soon," Espen muttered as Øyvin replied, "Chocolate."

I bit my lip at the slip up, but appreciated Øyvin's choice. I too loved any cookies with chocolate in them.

"Good evening, Solveig. May we have one of each to take home for dessert?" Espen asked the older woman. She was wearing a festive Norwegian knit sweater beneath her open jacket and a white-and-green nordic hat that knitters around the world would want to emulate.

"Merry Christmas," she replied in accented English, giving us her brightest smile as her eyes crinkled at the corners. "One of each coming right up." She grabbed a bag and tongs, and set to work. Her and Espen traded the bag for some cash after which she motioned for me to come closer and briefly ducked beneath the table, coming back up with a neatly wrapped gift.

She smiled at me and held out the parcel. "A little something for your first Norwegian Christmas."

My heart lodged in my throat as I accepted the present, remembering the woman's kindness when I'd first arrived in town.

"Go ahead, open it. It may come in handy," she said, and her little old lady friends, Jorunn and Dagny joined her, having finished up helping other customers. They both motioned to go ahead, their eyes wide with excitement, wool headbands pulled down over their ears and wispy white hair.

With trembling hands I gently pulled apart the paper, careful not to accidentally litter. My fingers brushed across a soft material and my breath caught for a beat. Inside was the most beautiful pair of mittens

I'd ever seen. White with an eight-pronged, red snowflake and the ends knitted into a point. The craftsmanship was immaculate.

"Thank you so much," I said, pulling them on and my hands instantly warmed. "They're gorgeous."

Solveig grinned, joy radiating off the kind woman. "You're welcome. I'm glad you like them."

Emotions clogged in my chest as I stared at the heartfelt gift, unsure what to say to express my gratitude for everything she'd done for me.

"Did you knit them yourself?" Øyvin asked, breaking the silence.

"I did indeed." Solveig nodded, before pointing to her friend, Dagny. "It's her pattern, but my handiwork."

"Very nice," Øyvin said, giving them all a congenial smile.

Espen agreed and with another thank you from me, we set off to see the rest of the town's festive setup.

As we stepped away from the white-haired trio, a blushing Dagny glanced over her shoulder and gave Øyvin a little finger-wave. To which he responded with a simple raised hand, and I bit my cheeks to stifle a laugh. I mean, don't get me wrong, I understood the appeal, and I couldn't blame her for trying to shoot her shot. But if she knew he was actually a fae... In fact, if she ever found out that Øyvin was more than a man, she might have a heart attack and die. So, it was probably best to leave her wanting and unknowing.

We meandered further into the throngs of people and Espen aimed for Fisken. On the street that ran beside the restaurant and up toward the main road through town, a couple of horse drawn carriages (in this case, sleighs with wheels put on them) with deer pelts covering the seats sat awaiting customers. The light beige horses whinnied and stomped their feet, their short and stick-straight white and black manes rustling.

"Norwegian Fjord Horses," Espen said, his warm breath tickling my neck as he leaned in close. "The breed has been around for eons, used by Vikings, too."

I scuttled closer to him and whispered back, "You mean they're older than Halvar?"

Espen snorted. "Not those horses in particular, but the breed? Most likely."

"You've known how old he is this whole time? I've been wondering—"

"No, no," he cut me off and pulled back, his eyes widened. "I have no idea how old Halvar is. I dare say, the only one who knows how old Halvar is, is the man himself."

Fair enough. The quest to figure out the ancient Fjell Fae's age continued. My current guestimate was somewhere in the 800s, but I could be wrong... Either way, I needed to find out what the guy's skincare routine was, because *damn*.

Two buildings down from the local restaurant, I spotted my favorite old curmudgeon serving up hot drinks at his stand and aimed in his direction.

Oddvar was busy and not one for small-talk, so we grabbed a hot chocolate each and a massive gingerbread heart—*pepperkake-hjerte*—with a stiff, swirly, iced sugar pattern piped onto it. The cookie was the size of my head, but tasted delicious and made a snapping noise when I took a bite.

While paying, Oddvar passed Espen an envelope and then glanced over at me. "Merry Christmas," he said with a curt nod. I replied swiftly with a "*God Jul*" having noticed the way Oddvar's lips had moved meant he hadn't spoken English. He nodded again and set back to work, assisting customers as they ordered their own hot chocolate and gingerbread hearts.

"Come on," Espen said with a pep in his step, his eyes wide with excitement. "The singing is about to start."

We joined the gathering masses as they crowded around the large evergreen, a bright white-colored star glowing atop it, and a little band started to play. The predominantly brass instruments sent echoing sounds around the harbor and the crowd began to sing, instantly recognizing the Norwegian song.

"And Christmas with the joyous and desire..."

Standing between my two guys, I winced and hunched my shoulders, refraining from being rude even though I wanted to clap my hands over my ears.

I'd finally found a fault with Nora's magic trickery that translated Norwegian for my brain.

Mass singing was a problem. A few of the words made orderly sense, but most of it sounded like jumbled words sprinkled with Norwegian. I cringed, wishing there was an on-off switch for it, but there wasn't. At least not one I knew of. I was doomed to listen to mismatched wording and an out of tune chorus.

Øyvin narrowed his eyes at me, then widened them and gave me a lopsided grin.

"Don't even."

"Don't what?" he pried, wiping his hand over his mouth and chin as if that would mask his glee.

"Enjoy this too much."

"We are so happy, so happy," the carolers continued, grinning from ear to ear. *"We are clapping, are clapping."* A second later, half the crowd—those most actively singing—spun in a circle, curtseyed, and bowed. My eyes bugged at the sight, wondering how a caroling event

could turn into a flash mob with flaming torches, all dancing in unison. Had Oddvar slipped something into the cocoa?

"Is Skolvik secretly a cult?" I asked, turning to Espen who was bobbing and clapping in time to the band.

He grinned and gave me a joking wink. "Only us *folk*. Do you not have songs like this back in America?"

I shook my head, staring out over the gathering while finishing off my gingerbread cookie with one large final bite. "Not quite like this."

Sure we had caroling events—often at churches or choral groups at theaters—but nothing similar. I was pretty certain this display of jubilation and tradition was what many of the Christmas markets around the world tried to achieve, but ultimately felt more like commercial cash-grabs with mulled wine that tasted like dog piss. Boiling wine really was an affront to the grapes—they didn't deserve that.

Espen bumped his shoulder against mine, glancing over with a smile that swiftly turned to a look of panic. "Your ears," he mouthed, his eyes wide as he quickly blocked my view of the stage.

Shit. Terror lanced through me, putting me on high alert, the cocoa shaking in my clutches.

Espen reached out his hand, aiming for my shoulder.

Øyvin grabbed his wrist from behind me and tossed it aside with a low growl. "Do it yourself," he bit out quietly, the words meant only for me. "Fix it."

Espen's worried gaze sent a shudder of fear through me. We were in public, in a huge crowd, and anyone could turn around right now or deviate their attention away from the carols and spot me and my fae ears.

A stuttered breath left my lips, panic taking over.

I couldn't expose the fae secret only a few months into becoming one myself. Halvar would kill me and then bury me somewhere deep within the mountain, probably in the tombs where they interred their dead. But I wouldn't get some fancy shrine-come-coffin with an effigy atop it like Queen Freija. No, no. I'd be deposited there in a nondescript stony box marked with: *Here lies the tourist-turned-demi-fae who betrayed our secret to an entire village of humans. On Christmas Eve, no less. Twenty-eight years old. Constant troublemaker. RIP.*

I shook off the maudlin thought and refocused. There was no use dwelling on that right now when I could still rectify the situation. I could do this. Espen nodded as if he could hear my thoughts, and Øyvin pressed his thumb and forefinger against my lower back providing an ounce of support.

I could totally do this. I just needed to focus and pull that magic swiftly up to my ears again.

I tugged lightly on my left earlobe, willing the power in my sternum to return to its spot, all while closing my eyes and picturing my non-pointy ears. The telltale warm energy swirled up my scarred arm, brushing through each prong of the lightning-shaped mark, and settled at my ear. I imagined it moving across to the other ear too, the warmth slowly following my request. I was putting on my magical earmuffs and it needed to stay there.

"Well done," Øyvin grumbled lightly behind me, rubbing a circle over my spine with his fingers before stepping back.

I opened my eyes to find Espen brushing his palm over his short beard and swallowing hard. "You did it. Now please keep it there or you'll give me an aneurysm." He stepped back beside me, exposing me to the crowd once more instead of blocking their view. Only a few people were peering in our direction, including Dagny, but they all swiftly looked back at the stage when I caught them.

Crisis averted.

A few songs later a woman with short white hair, wearing a long gray wool coat and authority that silenced the entire crowd, stepped onto a little platform in front of the tree. Thankfully, now that the singing had stopped, my Norwegian translation magic reverted back to its normal self, and I could understand what the woman was saying.

"Merry Christmas, Merry Christmas, and thank you all for being here this evening. On behalf of the mayor and—"

"That's my boss," Espen leaned down and whispered in my ear. "At least you didn't flash *her* with your ears."

I let out a single snort laugh. So, this was the chief of police. Part of me wanted to say hello, the more rational part knew not to go near the woman with my track record. In fact, it was probably best if I was never invited to any of Espen's work gatherings unless it was his fae job.

She continued her speech, wrapping up swiftly with more *God Jul*'s and reminders to grab cookies and goodies from the different stands. I was glad Espen had thought to grab some before the caroling began; with how many people were gathered here, there was about to be a post-singing rush on the cookie stands. I couldn't blame them. The treats looked delicious and I couldn't wait to try them later.

"You did it!" Espen exclaimed, fitting his hand in mine and swinging them through the cool night air as we sauntered along the deserted road just outside the village back to Øyvin's for dinner. "Not without hiccup, but you held the ear magic for ninety percent of the time!"

I shimmied my shoulders with joy and glanced back at Øyvin. "See, I'm not always a troublesome failure."

"Debatable," he huffed.

"You know what," I doubled down. "I think this deserves a reward." I wiggled my brows at Espen, hoping he'd get the hint.

"Dinner and presents first, then we can discuss any further rewards." He squeezed my hand and spun me in a circle as I let out a trill of laughter.

"I can work with that," I said, just as something landed on the tip of my nose. I stopped in my tracks and brushed my finger across it. Pulling my hand away from my face, I found a tiny snowflake clinging to the fibers of my new gloves. "It's—" I looked up and more flakes fell lightly across my cheeks. "It's snowing."

Espen chuckled and brushed his hand over his beard, taking in the whimsical scene unfolding around us, while Øyvin stepped up beside me, emitting a contented rumble from his chest.

"Snow for Christmas. It's been threatening frosty showers for weeks," Espen said, turning back toward the village behind us. "Look, Lennie."

Øyvin and I both spun around, and I sucked in a sharp breath.

We stood at the perfect spot on the road to capture Skolvik's beauty. Snowflakes fell gently across the town, dusting everything from the dark inky waters of the harbor, where boats bobbed and the lights from town shimmered across the ripples, to the Christmas tree and storefronts that sparkled under the glow of decorations.

The entire place looked like a snowglobe, and the magical scene took my breath away.

12

LENNIE

Logs popped and crackled in the stove fireplace, white lights flickered from the tree like fairies were hidden within the boughs, and the smell of a hearty home-cooked meal permeated the entire living room and kitchen, giving the boathouse a decidedly Christmassy feel.

Espen and I set the table when we got back from town, including little sprigs of fir and tealight candles in small glass votives dotted around the circular surface. Meanwhile, Øyvin carved the pork he'd roasted and completed the final preparations to his masterpiece—a meal, he'd mentioned, that was one of his favorites to cook. Dinner consisted of golden fingerling potatoes, pork belly with a crackling top, carrots, red cabbage, and a lingonberry jam that I wanted to smother over everything, including Espen.

Between trying everything and then sneaking one of Espen's favorite cookies—the *sirupsnippe* snapping then melting on my tongue—I was stuffed.

After helping wash dishes and put away leftovers, I practically rolled myself into the living room area. Curling up on the sofa, I tucked my feet beneath me and pulled one of the checkered throw pillows into my lap.

"Ready for some presents?" Espen asked, shoving an all-red santa hat onto his head.

"Ready!" I beamed, happy to see him happy, but still a little weirded out about opening presents on Christmas Eve. The Martin Family kids had been getting up to open presents at 7:00 a.m. on the dot for years, even when we were in high school and college. It had become a family tradition with all six of us in the living room, opening gifts together. By the time we were done, it always looked like a Hallmark store had exploded inside with wrapping paper and sparkly stick-on bows everywhere, the latter usually stuck all over Dad's head. That had shifted quite significantly post-college, but ever since my nieces were born, we were up early again, the adults chugging coffee to stay awake.

Espen leaned over and gave me a small satchel that fit in my palm.

"Is this from you?" I asked, shaking it lightly then tilting my head when a waft of something I couldn't quite name, but smelled herbaceous, drifted past my nose.

He shook his head. "That's from Heidi."

In that case...

I held the little pouch from the Forest Fae Healer further away from myself and lightly pulled at the drawstrings to open it. Nothing immediately jumped out, so I leaned in and pinched the fragment of parchment sticking out of the top. Unfurling the tiny piece of what looked like ancient papyrus, I read aloud the scrawling script, "For pleasure."

I scrunched my brow as I set aside the cryptic note. Reaching into the bag again, I pulled out a sachet of herbs and leaves and hell only knew what. It almost looked like a *ye olde poultice* that I'd seen on *Outlander*. "What the hell kind of tea bag is this?" I asked, holding it away from me, just in case the Forest Fae healer had decided to play a prank on me. I wouldn't put it past her as payback for the number of times I'd tried to bring coffee into her house in the forest.

Øyvin tilted his head and narrowed his eyes, but didn't move from where he perched on the piano bench, the sleeves of his navy sweater rolled up, exposing his forearms. Espen reached for the oversized gauzy tea bag and I handed it over for him to inspect. Lifting it to his nose, he took two short sniffs before a slow and steady smile grew on his lips.

"Not certain, but from what I can smell, this will make you feel all kinds of tingly and happy." He chuckled and handed it back.

"You mean it's weed?" I took a sniff. It didn't smell like weed. It smelled a hell of a lot nicer, but also earthy and somehow spicy, too. Green even, if green could be considered a smell. I placed the herb pouch back into the little gift bag and tightened the strings again before setting it on the coffee table.

"It's not marijuana, but it'll certainly make you feel good," Espen remarked, rolling his bottom lip between his teeth. "What did that note say: *for pleasure?*"

My stomach dropped and I looked between the two guys, eyes wide. "Holy shit! Is that for better orgasms?"

Øyvin snorted, but his eyes heated as they roved over me. Meanwhile Espen snickered, before giving in to a full-on belly laugh.

I chuckled, my cheeks hurting from smiling so much today. "Okay, don't laugh too hard." I jabbed my elbow into Espen's side. "You'll both be happy if that has me moaning your names in under two seconds."

They both stilled, and the air in the room heated—or maybe it was my body warming under their heady stares.

"You already moan our names in a few seconds," Øyvin said, leaning his elbows on his thighs, looking ready to launch himself at me to test the theory. Goosebumps skittered across my arms under his intense gaze. Yeah, I wouldn't mind taking things upstairs once we were done here.

"Before we try this out," Espen said, clearing his throat in the process. "This is from Oddvar." He pulled an envelope from his back pocket and handed it over.

I made a surprised noise, opened the envelope, and unfolded the piece of paper only to find that the letter was unreadable. "It's all in Norwegian," I said, furrowing my brow and attempting to read the first line, but failing spectacularly as my Norwegian comprehension wasn't that advanced.

"Let me see," Øyvin said, his hand outstretched.

I passed the letter to him for translation.

"Dear Lennie, I have taken your request under consideration,"—Øyvin scrunched his brow, and I realized I'd forgotten to tell them about my brief chat with the café owner—"and, while I feel you have much to learn, I wouldn't mind your assistance at the café this summer for the tourist season. Part-time. We start training in May. Merry Christmas, Oddvar."

My eyes widened and I looked between the two fae in slight bewilderment. *Had I just been offered a job?* My mouth hung open like a goldfish as I tried to come to terms with the contents of the letter. *Had that actually worked? Holy shit!*

I had to learn how to use the fancy Italian espresso machine. Would probably need to watch some videos online to learn how to use all the gadgets and gizmos… then learn all the names for all the different things in the coffee shop *in Norwegian*. I rose to my feet, clutching one of the throw pillows to my chest as realization dawned on me.

I had to basically be somewhat fluent in Norwegian… in five months. All oxygen left my body. Why hadn't I thought of that before asking

Oddvar about the job? "I need to learn Norwegian as fast as human-fae possible."

Someone tugged on my arm and I glanced down to find Espen staring up at me, his smile encouraging. "It'll be all right. We'll help you, won't we, Øyvin?"

I looked to Øyvin who peered up at me, his head tilted slightly to one side like he was preparing a challenging remark. But he shook his head, keeping whatever snark he'd planned to himself, and grunted, "Sure."

"Wonderful." Espen beamed and gently pulled me back onto the sofa where I settled in closer to him, curling up with my feet touching his thighs. "Now, onto the next presents."

If there was ever a time for Espen's quick subject pivoting tendencies, this was it. I didn't want to think too hard about the mess I'd inadvertently put myself in. Instead, I wanted to focus on enjoying my first Christmas Eve in Norway. My first festive season with these guys.

Our gift exchange continued and I opened a Norwegian wool sweater from the guys. It was white with a frosty-blue pattern across the top in the shape of snowflakes, and I couldn't wait to wear it.

I gave them both wooly hats, each with an obnoxiously large pom-pom on the top. I knew Espen would appreciate it, but Øyvin... Well, I just really wanted to see how much the thing irked him and if he'd actually wear it. Was he the kind of guy who would wear something once to be polite and then shove it into the back of a drawer to be forgotten about, or would he continue wearing it regardless?

"Try it on," I motioned to Øyvin who stared at the pom-pom with a flat smile. Espen meanwhile was already bobbing his head back and forth, the hat secure on his head and a grin plastered across his face. "Go on. I bet it'll bring out your eyes."

He gave me a deadpan stare, let out a deep sigh, and pulled the hat over his head. Tufts of blond hair stuck out the sides and a little across his forehead. "Happy?" he asked, his lips in a firm line but his eyes warmed as he looked over at me.

I clapped my hands together and brought them to my lips. "Ecstatic."

His mouth quivered into a miniscule lopsided grin, like he couldn't quite stop himself, and that alone made my heart beat a fraction faster.

"Well, that's it for presents," Espen exclaimed, shifting to face me on the sofa, and I broke my gaze from Øyvin's.

I peered across the little living room toward the tree. "What about that? Who's that one for?" I asked, nodding to the box wrapped in blue paper with silvery snowflakes on it. It was the only present remaining, shining like a beacon from beneath the twinkling tree in the corner.

"That's for tomorrow," Øyvin said as he pulled off his hat, stood, and offered me his hand. "Do you think you can wait that long?"

"Depends." I took his hand and rose from the sofa. "You two have any other festive activities you want to partake in this evening?"

Espen flicked his brows as Øyvin replied, "I'm sure we can think of a few."

13

LENNIE

"So," I started, stretching in my seat at the kitchen table, feeling sufficiently full from the leftovers we'd devoured for breakfast along with eggs. "What's the plan for today?" Normally, back in the US, after breakfast and presents we'd go on a walk in a park or watch movies with hot cocoa. "Please tell me there's no more caroling. Don't get me wrong, that was fun and a new experience for me, but I don't think my ears can handle translating more Norwegian singing."

Espen chuckled and planted a kiss on my forehead as he grabbed our plates and loaded them into the dishwasher. "How about the presents from us?"

"But you already gave me the sweater," I said, my voice a little wobbly as I hadn't got them two presents. The hats were it from me.

"This is your main gift from us," Øyvin replied. "The sweater was your Norwegian Christmas Eve present."

"What are you talking about?" I asked, rising from my seat and moving toward the Christmas tree, eyeing the last present we hadn't unwrapped last night. "That one?"

"Take a seat," Espen said, and I acquiesced without complaint, curling up on the sofa. Øyvin strolled over and took up his same spot from last night on the piano bench, his shirt sleeves rolled up to reveal his forearms. The sight, in itself, was a present. "First, this one." Espen plucked a tiny green velvet pouch that I hadn't noticed last night from one of the branches. He handed me the bag and plopped down beside me, the leather sofa sinking with his weight.

"Is this another gift from Heidi?" I asked, holding it at a safe distance just in case. Don't get me wrong, the 'tea' she'd gifted had been great—ten out of ten, would recommend. But I still didn't wholly trust the woman.

Espen shook his head. "This is from us, but isn't necessarily for Christmas."

Bringing the pouch closer, I scrunched my brows and untied the gold drawstring. *What on earth is this?*

I upended the bag over my palm. Something small and decidedly ring-shaped fell out, landing gently in my cupped hand. I swallowed around a lump that took up residence in my throat and eyed the piece as my heart rate picked up speed.

Holy shit.

"I-I..." I stuttered, unable to get the words from my brain to my mouth as I blindly set aside the empty bag.

In my palm was a stunning ring with a teardrop-shaped sapphire. The stone glinted from where it sat nestled between silver branches with tiny leaves on them. I may not have been a girly girl, nor very emotional—in fact my Dad often likened me to an ostrich with my head always in the sand when it came to feelings—but damn if I couldn't appreciate the sparkle and clear meaning behind the ring in my palm.

The branches and leaves on the engagement ring represented the Forest Fae and Espen, and the water droplet represented the Fjord Fae and

Øyvin. My heart thumped in my chest and my hand shook minutely as I stared at the tiny, beautiful object.

"If the powers that be in the human world need to believe we're really engaged, we figured it might be wise if you had a ring."

He was right. I'd agreed to marry Espen—for immigration purposes—but, based on the way my heart clenched as I looked between both of them, I suspected it might one day be more. Not that I was ready to fully and officially define the relationship, but... I shook my head.

This was bigger than just me. This was about the fae magic within me and the region and people that magic belonged to. I was both human and fae. A demi-fae who needed to learn how to fully control her powers. This fake engagement—*fae-gement* if you will—was necessary for so many reasons, and I was surprisingly okay with that.

Norway really was changing me. I'd gone from never listening to authority figures to obeying (sometimes), and now here I was committing to stay, not just for myself, but for others too. What was next? Would they anoint me as their Chosen One? Or vote me in as their leader? Only time would tell, I guessed.

The room remained silent, but as I slid the ring onto my finger, two relieved sighs drifted past.

"It's gorgeous," I remarked, shifting my hand and watching as the light from the kitchen and tree bounced off the facets of the sapphire.

"Good," Øyvin said, taking a deep breath, just as Espen replied, "I'm glad to hear it."

The latter jumped up from the sofa and went back to the tree returning with the final gift. "This is from both of us," Espen said, sidling up next to me again and handing me the box with the blue paper. "We hope you like it."

Tearing noises filled the room as I shredded the paper. Then my heart stopped beating.

"Wha—what?" I could barely get the word out, could hardly breathe. The world stopped spinning as I took in the sight of a brand new DSLR camera. "Guys."

"We thought you could use a new one," Espen murmured.

"Just don't take photos of fae areas," Øyvin added. Ever the dutiful and protective guard.

My hands trembled as I shoved aside the wrapping paper and opened the box. The new camera smell hit me—that odd aroma of cardboard, foam, and metal—and my heart started thumping again, quickening in pace.

They'd bought me a new camera to replace the one that had been destroyed by Nora. They'd known I couldn't afford to move out here *and* buy a new one, so they'd gone ahead and...

I couldn't even think straight. Tears welled in my eyes. I wasn't one for grand displays of emotion, but I couldn't hold back the happy tears as my lips curved into a smile. "Thank you so much."

Espen reached over and squeezed my thigh lovingly. "You're welcome."

I placed my hand over his and swept my thumb back and forth in gentle caressing motions. With a glance toward Øyvin, I found him smiling. He didn't need to say anything. For however grumpy the Fjord Fae could be, there was one thing I could always count on with him: he showed his emotions through his eyes. Right now, they were filled with a contented warmth that had me feeling loved.

We hadn't put any labels on this *situationship*, but through these gifts and all of their actions over the past few months, I could truly say they cared about me. A lot. And the feeling was mutual.

I let out a quick breath of air, and straightened up, not interested in getting even more emotional. Shifting my hand away from Espen's, I shut the lid with a contented sigh and let my heart rate settle down again, my mind drifting.

I wasn't entirely sure what the next five months would entail—except perhaps training with Halvar, but I didn't want to think about that frightening prospect right now.

In the meantime, I'd fill my days with practicing Norwegian so I could work with Oddvar this summer, hike with my new camera, and spend time with two guys whose company I was coming to adore and whose world I wanted to learn more about.

It was a commitment, but I wasn't worried about it. In fact, it might actually be nice to fully commit to something for once. Surprisingly, the thought of staying in Norway and making a life here wasn't daunting at all.

I glanced down at my sparkling left hand as it rested on the camera box. Thoughts of all the places we could go where I could take photos filled my head, all the nature I could capture, all the trips. A smile spread across my lips and my heart thumped happily in my chest.

I couldn't wait for the fun adventures this camera and I were about to go on.

REVIEW

Thank you for reading! I hope you enjoyed this little story. If you did, please consider leaving a review on Amazon or Goodreads!

Reviews are extremely helpful for indie authors, and I'd greatly appreciate your support!

Best wishes,
Elle

THANK YOU

Thank you to my readers!! You've made this writing journey an absolute blast and I'm so glad you're enjoying my stories.

Major thank you as always to my editor, the Goddess of Punctuation and Chaos, Aimee. I'm so glad we found each other.

Thank you to my husband. Carl, you're the best thing that's ever happened to me too.

About the Author

Hey! I'm Elle Thrasher, an author of romantic fantasy books.

My books are filled with relatable heroines, swoon-worthy heroes, lots of laughs, and locations that will give you wanderlust.

While I'm originally from the UK, and lived in Norway for seven years too, I now live in the US with my husband and one very fluffy dog. When I'm not writing, I can usually be found drinking a cup of tea, staring at my never-ending tbr, or taking a joke waaaaay too far.

Follow me on <u>Instagram</u> for updates and don't forget to sign up for my <u>newsletter</u> to receive behind-the-scenes info, bonus material, and details about upcoming books!

www.ellethrasher.com

ALSO BY ELLE THRASHER

The Cerulean Lazulum Series

(Romantic Suspense/Urban Fantasy)

Cavendish

Hawke

The Nordic Fae Series

(Romantic Fantasy)

The Fae of the Fjord

Christmas on the Fjord (Novella)

The Fae of the Forest

The Fae of the Fjell

9 798990 343313